THE Driftwood PROMISE

Books by Maren Ferguson

SEA GLASS COVE

The Abalone Shell

The Driftwood Promise

Books by Suzie O'Connell

NORTHSTAR ROMANCES

Northstar Angels

Mountain Angel

Summer Angel

Wild Angel

Forgotten Angel

Hammond Brothers

First Instinct

Twice Shy

Once Burned

Northstar Holidays

Mistletoe Kisses

Starlight Magic

TWO-LANE WYOMING

The Road to Garrett

www.marenferguson.com

THE *Driftwood* PROMISE

Sea Glass Cove
BOOK TWO

Maren Ferguson

SUNSET
Rose
BOOKS

Copyright © 2017 Suzie O'Connell

All rights reserved. No portion of this book may be copied, retransmitted, reposted, duplicated, or otherwise used without the express written approval of the author, except by reviewers who may quote brief excerpts in connection with a review.

This is a work of fiction. Names, characters, places, and incidents are either the product of the author's imagination or used fictitiously, and any resemblance to actual persons, living or dead, business establishments, events, or locales is entirely coincidental.

ISBN-10: 1981249559
ISBN-13: 978-1981249558

This one's for Trish Davis (a.k.a. Mom) and Gail Hickam Fines. I'm not sure I would've finished it without your support. Thanks for the "nagging."

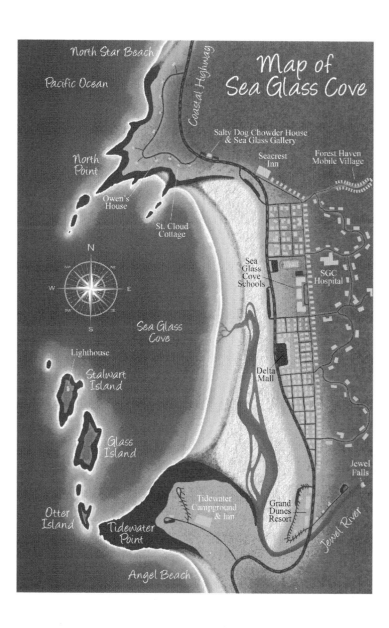

Map of
Sea Glass Cove

North Star Beach

Pacific Ocean

Coastal Highway

Salty Dog Chowder House
& Sea Glass Gallery

Seacrest
Inn

Forest Haven
Mobile Village

North
Point

Owen's
House

St. Cloud
Cottage

Sea
Glass
Cove
Schools

SGC
Hospital

N

NW   NE

W   E

SW   SE

S

Sea Glass
Cove

Lighthouse

Stalwart
Island

Delta
Mall

Glass
Island

Jewel
Falls

Otter
Island

Tidewater
Point

Tidewater
Campground
& Inn

Grand
Dunes
Resort

Jewel River

Angel Beach

One

THE SUN BURNED orange as it drifted closer to the ocean, and Erin paused in her paddling to bask in the glory of it. It had been unusually hot for the past week, but as day slipped into evening, the air stirred with a hint of a cool sea breeze. She couldn't imagine a more stunning evening to be out kayaking the cove with her brother. They'd paddled all the way down to the southern end of Angel Beach—three miles from home—and were just now passing by Tidewater Point and Otter Island, which divided Angel Beach from Sea Glass Cove. With their unhurried pace, they probably wouldn't reach Owen's truck until well after sundown.

"This was a marvelous idea, big brother," she remarked.

"I get them now and again."

"You ought to work on getting them more often." She beamed at him. "It's good to have you back."

He looked at her, squinting against the brilliance of the westering sun. "Let's not ruin a perfect evening by reminding me of when and why I wasn't so happy, all right?"

"As you wish. So… when are Hope and Daphne supposed to be getting back from Montana?" she asked.

"Tomorrow."

"Excited?"

His grin was all the answer she needed.

Erin started paddling again and steered her kayak toward Owen's, giving him a light bump. He regarded her with an amused smile and a brow lifted.

She wiggled her brows. "Race you back to the beach?"

"You want to race the full mile and a quarter?"

"Why not?"

"It's been a while, and we've been paddling all day."

"So?"

"All right." He shoved his paddle in the water and shot ahead with a powerful stroke.

He might have vastly superior upper body strength, but she'd been kayaking a lot more in the last three years, and her strokes were smoother, more efficient, and she had no trouble keeping pace with him as they rounded Glass Island and headed into the pass between it and Stalwart Island. The current flowing around the islands forced her to focus on her task, but thrill coursed through her veins and she crowed. As they reached the sheltered waters of the cove, she dug in harder and shot ahead.

"Come on, old man!" she called back. "Keep up!"

"Be careful what you wish for, little girl."

The ease with which he matched her pace even though he remained behind her made her nervous. He was toying with her, and as soon as they were within a quarter mile of the northern beach access, he hit the gas and zoomed past her. She scrambled to regain the lead.

They slid onto the sandy beach at the same time. Mirth erupted from her, and soon she was laughing too hard to crawl out of her kayak. Owen finally had to offer her a hand up.

"You great big turd," she said, still chuckling. "You played me."

"What?" he asked, grinning. "Did you seriously think I'd lost that much?"

She wrinkled her nose. "Maybe for a minute."

"Gotcha."

"Har har. You're hilarious."

He chuckled. "Come on. Let's get these up to the truck."

Movement at one of the houses on North Point caught her eye, and she glanced up to see a figure striding across the deck of the St. Cloud cottage. From the distance, she couldn't be sure if it was a man or woman. "I thought you said Hope and Daphne weren't going to be back until tomorrow."

"They aren't. She called from her parents just before we headed out in the kayaks. There's no way they could be back yet."

"Then who's that on the deck of the St. Cloud cottage?"

"Gideon must have come out early." Owen frowned. "But just in case, maybe we ought to stop by on our way up to my place."

"I hope it's Gideon."

"Do you now? I didn't realize he made such an impression on you at the summer solstice."

Erin rolled her eyes, but she didn't dare contradict him. He was plenty observant and would notice the hitch in her pulse. "What if it's a burglar?"

"We'll tie an anchor to his bootstraps and send him down to meet Davy Jones."

Erin hip-bumped him. "You know, I can't remember the last time you joked around like this. Remind me to thank Hope when she gets home."

They'd made better time across the cove than she'd thought they would, and as they carried the kayaks up the beach and through the sand dunes to the northern parking area, the ruby sun disappeared beneath the waves and the horizon darkened from molten yellow to the deep red of dying coals. Glancing again at the St. Cloud cottage as she strapped herself into the passenger seat of Owen's truck, she spotted an SUV in the drive-way—which she could see now, from this angle—and it looked familiar.

"That's Gideon's car, isn't it?"

"Looks like it."

"Guess we won't have to introduce anyone to Davy Jones tonight."

Erin rolled her window down and rested her head far enough over on the head rest for the wind to cool her face. Hot August nights indeed. Her eyes drifted closed and her lips curved. In this moment, cruising up the highway to North Point Loop with her brother, she was at peace with the world and everything in it.

"Yeah, that's Gideon's car," Owen said.

Without opening her eyes, she felt the truck slow and swerve before coming to a stop, and she guessed Owen had pulled over in front of the St. Cloud cottage.

"I know I said today was supposed to be a day for just us," he said, "but would you mind if I invite Gideon and Liam over to join us? It's the neighborly thing to do."

"I guess that'd be all right."

Owen climbed out of the truck, and as soon as his door closed behind him, she lifted her head and watched him stride around to the French doors at the back of the cottage. Why did no one use the front door of this place? Her eyes sought the living room window overlooking the driveway, hoping for a glimpse of Gideon, but the curtains were still drawn.

Owen returned quickly and slid in behind the wheel. "He's going to bring his bags in, and then he'll be over."

"They don't want to light the candles first?"

"I didn't ask, but Gideon didn't seem like he was in the mood to do it."

She only nodded, not trusting her voice to hide her intrigue at the prospect of seeing Hope's cousin again. As Owen had pointed out earlier, Gideon *had* made an impression during his brief visit back in June. More of an impression than any man since Chaz.

She sneered. She would *not* taint tonight by thinking of *him*.

"Hey, what's that look for?" Owen asked. "You want me to go back and rescind the invitation?"

"No," she replied quickly—probably *too* quickly. "That frown wasn't about him."

"Then what was it for?"

She sighed, closed her eyes again, and echoed what he'd said to her by Otter Island. "Let's not ruin tonight with memories of less happy times."

"I'm down with that."

She opened one eye. "What kind of man follows a phrase like 'rescind the invitation' with 'I'm down with that'?"

"One who's trying to erase that sneer from your face."

"Fair enough."

"I've got something that'll *really* wipe it off your face," he said, pulling into his driveway. "And I want to show it to you before Gideon comes over, so get your butt out of my truck. We'll get the kayaks later." The grin he flashed her was pure mischief. "Or maybe we'll leave them and go out again tomorrow."

"But Hope and Daphne will be home tomorrow."

"So? We've already planned a barbecue on the beach. Why not take Daph out in the kayaks, too? She hasn't been out in them yet. We could switch off— Hope and Daphne with me, Mom with Red… and Gideon with you."

Erin groaned. "Don't you dare think about playing matchmaker, Owen. I'm not looking to get involved with anyone. Ever."

"We'll see about that."

"I'm serious, Owen."

"So am I. You spent three years trying to pull me out of the shadows. It's only fair that I return the favor."

"Yeah… and you'll fail just like I did."

With bitterness seeping through her, she stalked ahead of him toward this front door.

"Hey." He grabbed her hand and spun her around to face him. "You didn't fail."

"Didn't I? It took meeting Hope to bring you out of it." Because her voice had a hard edge to it, she stood on her toes and wrapped her arms tightly around his neck. "And that's okay. I don't care what brought you out of it. I'm just glad to see you happy again."

"You ever think that maybe the reason you couldn't do it was because that part of me never broke?"

"Sure felt like it did."

She didn't mean to say it, and she winced when guilt darkened his handsome face. A sound that was part growl and part whimper rattled low in her throat. The grief of the last three years couldn't fade fast enough.

"I'm sorry, Erin," he murmured. "I never meant to shut you out."

"I know you didn't." She hugged herself. "Can we stop talking like this? Please?"

"Sorry. But, for the record, I was joking around— sort of. You're the one who took it—"

"All right! You win!" she groaned. "Just show me whatever it is you want me to see. Because the curiosity is killing me."

With a twinkle in his sea-green eyes, he held the door open for her. Unsure where he wanted her to go, she wandered into his dining room and slid her fingers over the two abalone shells sitting in the middle of his table. The smaller he'd found the day he'd met Sam. The larger had been the sign he'd needed to let go of the past and fully embrace his future with Hope… whatever it might bring. There was a third he'd kept hidden for three years that was now displayed beside his cash register in the Sea Glass Gallery, and she shuddered. The story of how he'd found that one chilled her.

Hugging herself, she looked around and realized he'd disappeared. "Owen?"

"Coming," he called from upstairs.

Moments later, he trotted into the dining room with a tiny box in hand. Her eyes rounded as he handed it to her. It didn't take too many guesses to figure out what was inside, but even though it was obvious, she inhaled sharply when she opened the box.

Cushioned on midnight blue velvet was one of the most exquisite and unique engagement rings she'd ever seen. It was traditional enough in shape—a smooth band of platinum that flared to embrace a round diamond—but it was what her brother had painstakingly laid into the channels beside the diamond that made it one-of-a-kind. The highly polished, iridescent abalone shell shimmered in the light of the chandelier over his table.

"Oh my God, Owen! This is gorgeous. And you made it entirely yourself?"

"Not entirely, but mostly. I had some help from Hoyt down at Sea Gems. It took me a few tries to get it right. I've never worked with platinum before."

"When are you planning to propose?"

"Don't know yet. I figured I'd give her some time to settle in first."

Erin briefly glanced at him, but her gaze was drawn like a magnet back to the ring. It was so true to her brother and so perfect for Hope that she couldn't find words adequate to describe the joy and the pride that swelled in her heart. Finally, she pushed the ring back into the protective velvet and set the box in his palm. She looked up at him. "This is a big deal, Owen."

"Yes, it is."

If she had ever doubted how he felt about Hope, the love that glowed in his eyes right now silenced it. And even as her happiness for her brother threatened to overwhelm her, the old bitterness crept back in. She had no idea what that felt like—that wonderfully consuming bond—but she craved it.

Right then, a knock sounded on the front door, saving her from the inevitable plunge into despair. Her brother jogged to answer it, and her lips curved. How could she be in danger of being lost to that relentless tide tonight? The promise of a bright future full of love and happiness for her brother drowned out everything else.

Moments later, Owen returned with Gideon on his heels, and Erin couldn't help it. She raked her gaze over him with one corner of her mouth lifted in feminine appreciation. With a neatly trimmed anchor goatee and rich, shoulder-length dark hair pulled back in a tail that reminded her a lot of Orlando Bloom's character in the Pirates of the Caribbean movies, Gideon St. Cloud was a delectable distraction. And those eyes, so dark and warm…. They threatened to swallow her. His frame and bone structure, lighter and more angular than her brother's, might be the product of his St. Cloud genes, but the darker coloring that set him apart from Hope and her daughter was entirely the gift of his Spanish grandmother.

"Gideon, you remember my sister Erin?"

"I do indeed." He took her hand and bowed over it, pressing a knightly kiss to her knuckles. "*Buenas noches, bonita.*"

"Yes, it is a good evening," she remarked, trying not to snort at his flirtatious greeting. She was pretty enough, but she'd never dream of calling herself a beautiful lady. That description she reserved for her mother, her late sister-in-law, and now Hope. Besides, if she were to give even half a second's thought to his endearment, she'd have to admit how it affected her.

Then she noticed a weariness in his eyes that sharply contrasted the gleam of merriment she remembered from their first meeting. He was hiding it, but not well. The desire to mock his greeting vanished. Softly, she said, "Welcome home to Sea Glass Cove, Gideon."

"Thank you. This is going to sound really pathetic, but when Owen stopped by and asked if I wanted to join him and you…." He shook his head. "You guys make me feel exactly what you said—like I'm coming home. I need that right now."

Whoa. This was nothing like the Gideon she'd met at the summer solstice party. That Gideon had laughed and cracked joke after joke, seemingly without a care in the world. If she remembered right, it had been over eight months now since he'd broken up with Hannah—he'd called it quits right about the same time Hope's divorce had been finalized. That was plenty of time to adjust to bachelorhood, so why was he worse now than he had been in June?

"Where's Liam?" she asked. "I thought Hope said he'd be coming out with you."

"That was the plan. Hannah changed it. Again."

"So it's just you and the dog?"

He nodded.

"For how long?" Owen asked.

"Not a clue. Maybe until our custody hearing." Gideon snorted. "Maybe never. She's refusing to agree to anything in the plan I came up with, so God only knows which of us will end up with custody of Liam."

"When's the hearing?"

"Almost a month away—the first of September."

The shift in his expression toward black despair made Erin uncomfortable, and suddenly, she thought it might be a good idea for her to head home so he and her brother could talk, man to man. "I'm sorry," she said quickly. "I should probably go. It's my day to open the restaurant tomorrow, and after our exertions today, I could probably use... the... rest."

The blatant plea in those dark eyes stole the breath from her lungs.

"Please don't go," he said quietly.

She was torn. Habits as old as she could remember had her itching to get away, but she couldn't ignore the inexplicable and potent reluctance to disappoint him. She glanced—as she often did—to her brother for reassurance.

"It's not *that* late yet, sis," he replied with a gentleness that belied his casual words.

He knew her better than anyone, but since the accident, he hadn't had the energy or focus or whatever it was that allowed him to sense even the tiniest shifts in her mood, and to see that insightful intensity back in his gaze again now was a jolt. He sensed her uncertainty, and that did a lot to alleviate it. Then it occurred to her that uncertainty wasn't the only thing he was likely to sense now that he wasn't so lost in his grief, and her heart accelerated. How much longer was he going to be satisfied with her vague explanation of why she'd left Chaz?

"Besides," he continued, "I thought we were going to stay up and watch the stars come out."

She shifted her gaze to Gideon. The way he held her gaze, begging her to stay....

He needed something from her. What, she had no

idea, and she doubted he did, either. That scared her. A jesting, nonchalant man she could handle, but one fighting an emotional battle that tugged at her heart-strings was dangerous. She was alone for a reason, even if watching her brother fall in love with Hope tempted her to forget that.

"Fine," she said with dramatic exasperation. "I'll stay a bit longer."

"Don't make me twist your arm or anything," Gideon teased.

The return of some of the playfulness that had captured her attention at their families' summer solstice party made it easier to reach into her brother's fridge and pull out the pitcher of lemonade. She grabbed three glasses and filled them.

"No arm twisting necessary," she said as she handed a glass to Gideon and nodded her head toward Owen's deck.

The men followed her outside, and she perched a safe distance away on the railing while they took seats at the glass-topped table to enjoy a cold lemonade on a sultry night. Erin studied Gideon covertly, but he seemed to have pushed his worries away for the time being, and she let out a breath. As much of a relief as it was to see him smiling again—even if some of the twin-kle was missing from his eyes—she couldn't quiet the sympathy triggered by his vulnerability. It was the same ache she'd felt deep in her soul watching her brother suffer.

Sighing, she took a long drink of lemonade. I hope I don't end up regretting not walking away when I had the chance.

Two

GIDEON STRETCHED HIS LEGS out in front of him, crossing them at the ankles, and knitted his hands behind his head. As twilight deepened and the stars began to appear, winking against the indigo, the day's heat finally abated, chased out by a cool sea breeze. Around Owen's deck, flames danced in the half dozen lanterns fixed to the railing. It wasn't the same as when he or Hope or Christian lit dozens of candles and lanterns on the deck of their family's cottage the first night home, but it reminded him of it. Maybe tomorrow, when Hope and Daphne returned from Montana, he'd be able to indulge in that magical tradition. He just couldn't bring himself to do it tonight. Not without Liam.

He reached for his lemonade, drained the rest of

it, and set the empty glass back on the glass-topped table.

He shifted his gaze to Owen's sister, who was currently perched several feet away on the railing, gazing across the ocean. What a stunning picture she made with the blue-green twilight as an exquisite backdrop and the warm glow of a nearby lantern outlining the contours of her face. Suddenly, he wished he'd thought to bring his camera.

A light flickered in the gloom of his mind—a delicate spark of interest. As soon as he acknowledged it, it flared to life, brighter than it had at their first meeting on the summer solstice. What was it about Erin McKinney that had captured his attention that night and held it every day since? With long, sun-gilded brown hair, a youthful face, and a toned, athletic body, she was beautiful. But so was Hannah. His ex was stunning, in fact, and if she was of a mind to cash in on it, she could be gracing the covers of magazines, maybe even the silver screen.

No, there was something else about Erin that drew his attention. It was her eyes. The same blue-green as the sun-caught barrel of a wave, they exuded innocent delight but were also tempered by the shadows of some deep-seated wariness. Right from the moment Owen had introduced them, he'd sensed that she was hard to get close to, that she liked to keep people at arm's length. Maybe it was the challenge of peeling back her defenses that so appealed, but he doubted it.

Abruptly, he turned his gaze higher, toward the glittering stars. He drew the thick coastal air deep into his lungs and let it out in a contented sigh. "God, I love it here."

"Are you seriously thinking about moving here?" Owen asked. "Hope said you were considering it."

"I am. I have so many fond memories of this place. I'd love for Liam to grow up here and make his own."

As soon as he mentioned his son, he wished he hadn't. The familiar ache returned, and he winced. He glanced at Owen and found sympathy in the other man's gaze, but rather than easing that ache, the reminder of what Owen had lost did the opposite. Even without Liam here to need a playmate, it was weird not having Sean around. And Samantha... Generous, incredible Sam.

He mourned their beautiful souls. He couldn't say he'd known them *well*, but he and Hannah and Liam had spent enough time with Owen and his family that he thought of them as his friends. With their house just two doors away from his family's cottage, it was only natural that the two men, who were the same age and had sons the same age, would come together.

Of course, looking back, spending time with them hadn't always been beneficial. Next to Sam's confidence and graciousness, Hannah's juvenility had been more apparent than ever.

And that day Sean and Liam had slipped down to Hidden Beach by themselves? Three and a half years later, the memory still infuriated him. Hannah was supposed to have been watching them while Gideon helped Owen and Sam cook dinner. Sensing something wasn't right, he'd walked out on the deck to check on the boys and had found her sitting at the very table where he sat now, texting her sister and oblivious to the fact that her son and their friends' son had vanished.

Gideon had never been so panicked in his life, and after they'd found the boys safe and sound building rudimentary sand castles, he'd laid into Hannah for her irresponsibility. She'd bawled, of course, and he'd felt guilty afterward, but that day had been a turning point for him. He hadn't trusted her with their son since.

After that, it had been impossible to ignore—no matter how much he wished it weren't true—that Hannah was more like Liam's apathetic older sister than his mother. She'd gotten pregnant at twenty only a few weeks after they'd started dating, and he wished he could blame her age. But he couldn't anymore. She was twenty-eight now, plenty old enough to step up and start acting like an adult.

"All right. I'm hungry," Owen announced, rising from the table. He snatched Gideon's empty glass. "That picnic lunch Erin and I had in the kayaks wore off a while ago, so how about I bring out some snacks?

Gideon, you hungry?"

He started to say no, but his stomach had other ideas. "Actually, yes, I could eat. Thanks."

Owen walked over to his sister to take her empty glass, and for almost a minute after he went inside, Gideon thought Erin planned to remain silent. Then she hopped down from the railing, sauntered over, and settled into the chair Owen had vacated.

"You're sure you don't want me to leave?" she asked. "I'd understand if you did."

"Positive. Why would I want you to go?"

"I don't know. I thought maybe you'd want to talk to Owen alone. Discuss father things."

"I enjoy your company as much as your brother's, you know. And to be honest, talking with a woman who isn't making my life a living hell might be rather beneficial."

She lowered her gaze to the table. He couldn't be sure if it was shyness or something else that made her do it, but he smiled. "I appreciate your concern. And your compassion. It's refreshing."

Frowning, she lifted her eyes to meet his again. "I can't imagine how hard this must be."

"It's not like she wants to be a parent, so I don't get why she's fighting me for custody," he muttered, unsure if he was talking to himself or asking for Erin's opinion. "I wasn't ready to be a father, and certainly not with her, but that's what happened. Life throws you a curveball, and you deal with it."

"You think she's doing this to spite you?"

"I *know* she is. She's making everything as difficult as she can. I wouldn't care if she did it behind closed doors where Liam couldn't see, but she's doing it in front of him."

He dragged his hands over his face.

"Is that why Liam didn't come with you?"

Nodding, he dropped his hands into his lap and hunched over his legs. "She knew I'd be coming home today, but when I got to her apartment to get him, she wasn't home. So I called her, and she told me she and Liam were already at her sister's in San Francisco. She wanted to head down earlier than planned. Okay, fine. Why didn't she call me so I could swing by the city and get him on my way home? It was out of my way, but not *that* far out. And why did she want to take him with her, anyhow? He hates going to his aunt's house, and I can't blame him. Emma's always been pretty nasty to him."

With anger tightening its grip around his chest and making it hard to breathe, he tipped his head back. Closing his eyes, he drew as deep a breath as he could and let it out. "Tell me she isn't being spiteful. And since I don't have a court order that says she has to bring him back, there's nothing I can do about it. Oh, she'll get tired of him soon enough and expect me to drop everything and go get him."

"And you will because he's your son and he needs

you."

He lifted his head again and nodded, his eyes locked on the lantern flickering beyond Erin's shoulder. "She acted like it was such an inconvenience to take Liam for a week while I went down to San Diego to shoot my cousin's wedding, and she made me out to be the bad guy. I already felt bad enough, but it wasn't something I could bring him to. And even if I could have, he would've been absolutely miserable. No kids, just a bunch of drunk adults. Plus two days in the car each way, me running around taking pictures all day for three days straight, and a god-awfully uncomfortable couch or the floor to sleep on."

"Hey, you don't have to explain yourself to me. You shouldn't have to explain yourself to her, either," Erin remarked. "She should *want* to spend time with her son."

"She should, but I'm not going to hold my breath. I'd die of asphyxiation long before that happened. She's made it too clear too many times that she has no desire to play Mommy. Which, fine, I get that. But she *is* a mother, and she needs to either let me have him or step—"

He snapped his mouth closed.

It was like she'd flipped a switch. Her demeanor shifted *that* quickly from sweet sympathy to delightful mischief.

"Is that why you still have the Will Turner vibe

going on?" she asked. Her eyes sparkled merrily and her lips twisted into a smile that dared him to resist. "To spite her back?"

Gideon relaxed into his chair, surrendering to his companion's well-timed and intuitive mood shift. There was that shy sense of humor he remembered from his too-short visit in June. The spark flared again, and despite himself, he chuckled. "Maybe a little bit. It's grown on me, though."

"Literally and figuratively. And Liam likes it, as I recall."

He narrowed his eyes with the smile still curving his lips, surprised she remembered that. "He said I have to dress up as a pirate for Halloween this year."

"You could totally pull it off."

He tilted his head. "Is this your idea of flirting?"

She sat up. It was a subtle shift in position, but noticeable enough to catch his attention and tickle his curiosity.

"I don't flirt."

Despite her comment, there was a gleam in her expression that straddled the line between friendly and flirtatious. She was a fascinating blend of innocence and confidence, and while he'd come across that combination before, she was different somehow.

"My apologies," he said.

"For what?"

"Upsetting you. I didn't mean to unload on you

like that, but you're very easy to talk to."

"So I've been told. And you haven't upset me. I'm happy to listen." She flashed him another smile. "I'm just not a flirtatious person. Never have been."

"Then you fooled me at the summer solstice."

"That wasn't flirting. That was...."

He waited at least fifteen seconds for her to finish her thought, but she only stared through the windows into the kitchen where her brother was plating something that looked a lot more elaborate than anything Gideon would term "snacks."

"That was what?" he pressed, turning back to Erin.

She met his gaze, and the warmth in her eyes was so inviting and poignant that his pulse accelerated. Another shift in mood, another glimpse into her intriguingly multi-faceted spirit.

"That was me being giddy for my brother. Do you know that Hope is the first woman he's dated since Sam died?"

"I didn't. Doesn't surprise me, though. It'd take a long time to move on after a woman like Sam. But my cousin's a good woman, too."

"Yes, she definitely is. I'm glad they found each other."

"Me, too."

Silence fell over the deck, disturbed only by the peaceful rhythm of the waves braking lazily against the bluffs. It wasn't the kind of quiet he felt the need to fill with chatter. Rather, he was content to enjoy Erin's company and the fondness for her brother that radiated from her. There was something else about her, something he sensed more than observed, and it was in the way she sat, so still and alert even when contentment radiated from her, like she was savoring the moment with all five senses. She was constant, and it sharply contrasted his ex's hummingbird-like flitting.

She regarded him with a brow lifted. "Find me fascinating?"

"Riveting."

"Uh-huh," she remarked slowly, angling her head like she either didn't believe he was serious or didn't believe he could find her interesting.

Owen returned then with the snacks—coconut shrimp, a veggie tray, and cheese and crackers—and refills. Perfect timing. Erin accepted her glass and drank the contents with a speed that spoke of someone preparing to make a hasty exit. Gideon wasn't surprised when she rose from her chair just moments after finishing her lemonade. She piled a few shrimp in her hand and gave them a polite but shallow smile.

"It's been a fantastic day," she said, "but I really do need to head home. Five AM isn't that far away. It was great seeing you again, Gideon."

"Likewise," he replied.

"See you on the beach tomorrow evening?"

"Absolutely."

She leaned down to hug her brother and kiss his cheek, and then she vanished down the stairs of the deck and into the night. Gideon stared at her empty chair long after he heard her car start and drive away. Why did it feel like she'd taken the evening's warmth with her?

Across from him, Owen watched him with an amused gleam in his eyes, tapped his fingers idly on the rim of his glass, clearly wanting to say something. Gideon took a long drink of his lemonade and waited.

He didn't last thirty seconds before curiosity got the best of him.

"All right, spill it. What are you thinking?"

"Just wondering what you said to my sister while I was in the house."

"You think something I said chased her off?" he asked, afraid that it might be true.

"Something like that."

Gideon slumped and folded his arms on the table. "I said a lot more than I planned to. About Hannah. You think that made her uncomfortable?"

Owen shook his head and sipped his lemonade, but he never took his eyes off Gideon. "Uncomfortable isn't the word I'd use. Not in the way you're thinking."

"Then how?"

"She was excited to see you tonight. She tried to hide it, but she was."

He started to ask how *that* would make her uncomfortable, but he already knew. She preferred to keep people at a safe distance, and there was undoubtedly a reason why. It was tempting to ask Owen what that might be, but he didn't want to cheat. Wasting so many years of his life trying to hold on to a hollow relationship had shown him beyond a doubt that he wanted more, and the clues he'd been picking up since June made him believe Erin might be exactly that. More. She might even have the capability for the kind of deep, lasting love that had prevented his father from remarrying after his wife's death in childbirth. That's what he wanted—a love so consuming it would fuel his heart for the rest of his life and beyond.

"I want to ask her out," he admitted, "but now's the worst possible time. I'm in the middle of a custody fight that shouldn't even *be* a fight, for God's sake."

"But...?"

Gideon hunched over his knees again for a moment while he gathered his wits. When he straightened again, Owen looked at him expectantly. "She made me laugh tonight when I shouldn't have been able to. I can't ignore that. And she's...."

More than a minute passed in silence as he wrestled the words to explain what he felt when he wasn't even sure why he felt it. All he knew was that something had happened in June when he'd watched Erin building that elaborate driftwood fort with Liam and Daphne.

Liam hadn't stopped talking about it since, and it was never the fort at the center of his praise.

"She's what?" Owen prompted.

"She's a big part of the reason I finally filed for custody of Liam."

Three

"HEY, BIG BROTHER."

Owen dropped his spoon in his clam chowder. "That's it. I'm eating in my office from now on."

Erin rolled her eyes at his teasing. "Oh, come on. I'm not that bad."

"Yes, you are."

She stuck her tongue out at him. "You're mean. I just wanted to know what you and Gideon talked about after I left last night."

"Do you now."

"Well, don't you always say I have a bad habit of pushing people away?"

"You do."

"Well, it seems to me Gideon could use a friend

right now, and he's a nice guy, and… maybe I don't want to push him away."

"You want to know if he's interested in you," Owen surmised.

"At the risk of sounding like a silly high school girl… is he?"

"Took you long enough."

She regarded him with a brow raised. "Took me long enough to what?"

"Act like a silly high school girl. Though I suppose I should thank you for that. Saved me from having to go big brother on the boys who wanted to date you. Except that one time…."

"Yeah, except that one time," Erin murmured. "When Toby Dahlquist decided he wanted to get laid on prom night and wouldn't take no for an answer. He's still terrified of you, you know."

"I can't say that breaks my heart." Owen used a piece of sourdough to mop up the dregs of his clam chowder.

"So, back to Gideon," she said.

"You already know the answer to that question."

"If I knew, I wouldn't ask."

"Riveting, I believe, was the term he used to describe you last night when you asked him if he found you fascinating. He also told me that you made him laugh when he shouldn't have been able to."

He tucked his arm around her waist and drew her

down onto his leg for a hug. More out of habit than a need for comfort, she rested her head on his shoulder. God, she'd missed this—these little moments of closeness with the man who had been her rock since their mother had taken them and fled their abusive father.

"He's a good man, Erin," Owen murmured. "Certainly better than Chaz. Give him a chance, all right?"

She winced. It wasn't difficult to be a better man than Chaz, but Owen didn't know that. "I thought you liked Chaz."

"Not nearly as much as I've always liked Gideon. At best, Chaz was just all right."

"Then why didn't you talk me out of moving to Santa Barbara with him?"

"You had your heart set on it." He sighed. "You ever going to tell me what happened between you two?"

"We just… grew apart." The lie tasted sour, but she leaned back in his arms and gave him her brightest smile. Brows drawn together—he wasn't fooled. "Someday. After you and Hope are married and that godawful week is so far behind us it won't hurt to talk about it. Deal?"

"Deal."

The bell on the door of the Salty Dog Chowder House jingled, and Erin glanced over her shoulder, prepared to bounce to her feet to greet either her afternoon waiter, who was late, or another table of customers. It wasn't either, and she grinned. "Good. Because guess who just walked through the door."

At once, he turned on his stool, and his expression shifted from mildly exasperated amusement to the brightest, most amazing smile she'd seen on his face in a long time. Hope and her daughter Daphne were just stepping inside, and their faces matched Owen's perfectly. It was such an incredible thing, that dopey, beautiful love. Erin grinned and nudged her brother with her elbow, but he was already rising to his feet.

"Go get 'em," she murmured fondly.

She headed into the kitchen to ladle some chowder into sourdough bowls—Hope's and Daphne's favorite. When she returned, her brother had both his ladies locked in his embrace. Not wanting to disturb them, she set the clam chowder beside her brother's and stepped away to check on her customers. Try as she might, she couldn't help glancing frequently at the threesome.

Hope would say yes when Owen got around to proposing. Erin was certain of it. A woman didn't glow like that unless she was totally in love. And Daphne.... She couldn't wait to call that oh-so-sweet little girl her niece.

"It's a beautiful thing, isn't it?"

Erin nearly dropped the load of dishes she was taking back to the kitchen. Not trusting herself to keep hold of them, she set them on the counter and turned to Gideon with her palm over her thumping heart. That lop-sided grin was adorable, and she laughed softly despite the adrenaline still singing through her veins. "Don't *do* that! You scared the bejeezus out of me."

"Sorry."

She noted the smug satisfaction playing about his lips and snorted. "No, you aren't."

"All right, I'm not. You're adorable when your response isn't rehearsed."

She lifted a brow. "What's that supposed to mean? And what's a beautiful thing?"

"It means that you're a very guarded person. And *that*'s a beautiful thing," he replied, tilting his head toward Owen, Hope, and Daphne.

"Mmm. It is."

He chuckled, and the way those dark eyes glittered made her heart skip a beat. She took a step back, glancing into the kitchen to see if her mother had the fish and chip baskets for her last table ready. As soon as those guests were done, she was done for the day… if her waiter decided to show up.

"I wish I knew why."

"Why what?" she asked, turning back to him.

The humor was gone from his eyes, replaced by a tender smile that was even more disarming than the smarmiest grins he'd lavished her with in June.

"Why you don't flirt and why you have such high walls."

"Why do you care?"

The question was out of her mouth before she had time to consider how rude it sounded.

"For one, I try to be a good friend. For another…. It's like I told your brother last night after you left. You made me laugh when I shouldn't have been able to, and that intrigues me. *You* intrigue me."

Erin started to say she wasn't nearly as interesting as he seemed to think, but the words refused to come. Instead, she ducked her head to hide the shy smile and the blush that warmed her cheeks. "I need to check on my customers," she mumbled.

She made her circuit of the dining room, aware that she was using her job to distract herself from the implications of Gideon's remarks. By the time she made her way back to the kitchen, her mother was setting the fish and chip baskets in the serving window, and that gave her a few more minutes to figure out what she wanted to do. He was attractive—there was no point in denying that—and she liked his sense of humor even though there was a probing quality to it that made her nervous. She also adored his love for his son and ached for the pain the custody battle brought him.

Maybe she didn't have to decide anything. Maybe she just needed to let go and let the tides take her where they would. That seemed to be working out well for Owen and Hope.

Her brother was right, that she had a bad habit of pushing people away. Especially men. With her thirty-first birthday now behind her, it was time to admit that going through life like this wasn't any way to live. It was lonely. Her relationship with Chaz had given her a taste of the kind of companionship that could keep two people together for a lifetime, and even though it hadn't lasted, she hadn't been able to forget the feeling.

"Jeff still isn't here?" her mother asked her when she slipped into the kitchen with another load of dirty dishes.

"Nope."

"When he shows up, you make sure he knows this is his last chance."

Erin nodded. She hated to give the kid an ultimatum because he was great with the customers, and he was efficient and worked hard. But this was the third time in the two weeks since he'd started that he'd been late… and not just a few minutes late. Half an hour or more late.

The bell on the door jingled just before Erin returned to the counter where Gideon was currently engaged in conversation with his cousins and Owen, and she glanced toward it and frowned. Jeff strolled inside with his blond hair still damp.

Erin glanced at her watch and made sure he saw her do it.

"I'm sorry I'm late," he said when he reached her.

"Again," she added. "You were supposed to be here at noon, Jeff. It's now a quarter to one."

"Sorry, Erin. I really am."

"You were out on the beach with your friends again this morning."

"Yeah…. We lost track of time. Sorry."

"That's the third time you've said you're sorry. Show up to work on time and you wouldn't have to say it at all. Don't be late again."

She held his gaze to make sure her meaning sunk in.

He nodded vigorously. "Understood."

"Good. Get to work. You get any new tables that come in."

"Yes, ma'am. And I'll start clearing your tables while I wait."

"That would be wonderful. Thank you."

The last fifteen minutes of her shift kept her busy chatting with her guests and ringing up their meals, and it didn't give her much time to continue her ponderings about Gideon. That was probably for the best, given her tendency to overthink… everything. Thanks to Jeff clearing the tables for her, she clocked out on time. She was inclined to be grateful to him for stepping up to make up for his tardiness rather than focus on the fact that she would've had fewer tables and plenty of time to do all that herself if he'd shown up on time. It was a gorgeous day—almost as hot as it had been yesterday—and the promise of an evening on the beach with her family and Hope and Daphne and, yes, Gideon, too, and his goofy black Lab put her in a fabulous mood.

At last, she rejoined her brother and his companions with her mother in tow so they could discuss their plans for the evening.

Andra immediately embraced Hope and Daphne, and then turned to Gideon and gave him a hug, too. "Wonderful to see you again, Gideon. Where's your boy?"

"With his mother."

The pain that shadowed his smile made Erin's chest tighten, and she almost reached to give his hand a squeeze. Almost.

"Any news on the custody front yet?"

"No, ma'am. We have a hearing on the first."

"Well, if you need anything at all, you let us know."

"Thank you. I appreciate that."

"All right," Owen said. "How are we going to get everything together for tonight?"

"I can get most of it," Erin offered. She turned her gaze on Gideon and grinned.

"Why are you looking at me like that?" he asked slowly, glancing between Erin and Owen.

"Well, since Hope and Daphne *just* got back into town while you've had all night and this morning to get settled, and since both Mom and Owen will be here until five—" She took a deep breath. Could she really do this? Could she open the door to him? "—that leaves you."

"Leaves me what?"

"As the only available pack mule. You can help me haul the food and coolers down to the beach."

"Do I have a choice?"

The gleam in his eyes contradicted his words, so she called him on it. "Do you want one?"

He caught the meaning behind her words—the unspoken invitation—and strolled right through that open door with a broad grin. "Nope."

"I need to run home to see what I need to pick up at the grocery store. All that and shopping shouldn't take me more than an hour, if you want to meet me at my house around two."

"Why don't I come with you?"

She hesitated, then chided herself for her habitual rejection of assistance. An extra pair of hands would be useful. Given her response so far to the man attached to those hands, it would likely be pleasant, too. "Sure, if you don't mind."

From the corner of her vision, she caught Owen glancing between her and Gideon with his brows lifted and his lips curved in amusement.

"What?" Erin asked her brother.

He shook his head, but his smile turned smug. "Nothing."

She lifted her brows. *"Nothing" my butt.*

She wasn't ready to dive into the scheme certainly

percolating in her brother's brain, so she kept her mouth shut.

Gideon dug his keys out of his pocket and handed them to Hope. "Would you mind letting Shadow out to potty, and then bring her down to the beach with you? Oh, and would you bring my camera and my guitar, too?"

"Just that?" Hope asked. Her lips twitched.

"Well, I suppose we might need the kitchen sink…."

"Dog. Camera. Guitar. I think I can manage that. Mind if I take your car? I don't think I can fit all that in mine until I get all our stuff unpacked, and I won't get to that until tomorrow."

"Help yourself. Thanks, cuz. See you on the beach."

Erin touched Gideon's shoulder and inclined her head toward the door. He gestured for her to lead the way and followed her out of the restaurant.

"I'm not sure I would've been as nice to my employee for showing up so late," Gideon remarked as they climbed into her car. "You were firm but fair. Impressively so."

"Thanks," she said, unable to stop the smile that spread across her face at his praise. "He's a good worker."

"A good worker is useless if they aren't reliable."

"True. And this was his last get-out-of-jail-free

card."

"I hope he appreciates that."

"I hope so, too. He's a good kid."

"So, is it just you and your mom and Jeff running the place?"

"No, we have another cook—Zach—and two waitresses—Lily and Zoey. It's just Mom and me running the business end of things, though."

"That's fun—a mother-daughter operation. And Owen has his gallery in the same building. You guys have a wonderful bond. Not every family can work together like that."

"We do," Erin agreed. "But we've had to rely on each other. It's been just the three of us since I was six. Well, until Mom finally agreed to a date with Red. But by then, Owen and I were both adults, so the foundation was already laid. What about you? I've only heard about you and your dad."

She turned onto Forest Haven Road. After a hundred yards, it slipped into the cool, dense forest and snaked up the hill toward the mobile home village she'd called home for the last twenty-five years.

"It's been just the two of us most of my life. My mom and baby sister died in childbirth when I was six, and after that, Dad and I moved to the Puget Sound to be closer to his side of the family."

"I'm so sorry to hear that. What a heartbreaking thing. He never remarried?"

Gideon shook his head, and the poignant smile—the way it shone in his eyes more than his face—changed him from handsome to outrightly beautiful. It wasn't a term she'd associate with any man but her brother, but it fit. "He used to say that his heart beat only for my mother and that no other woman would ever be able to take her place."

"I was beginning to think that might be the case for Owen, too, until he met Hope."

"I think Dad would've remarried if he'd found the right woman," Gideon remarked thoughtfully. "He just hasn't found her yet. And if he doesn't, he'll be happy to have loved my mother."

"What a beautiful thought."

And it was. The idea that such love existed kindled a glow in her heart that was as much hope as wonder. She *knew* it existed; she'd seen it with her own eyes every day of her brother's marriage to Samantha, and she'd seen it blossoming again between Owen and Hope over the last couple months. She'd also seen it between her mother and Red, even though she'd been too caught up in her own heartbreak to pay it much attention at first. But to hear evidence of it beyond her own family was something different. It made such a love more than a fluke. It made it something that could happen to anyone… even her.

They'd reached the gate of the Forest Haven Mobile Village, and she slowed to adhere to the ten-mile-an-hour speed limit and to avoid jarring them too badly on the speed bumps.

"That first trailer there—that's the one we moved into when Mom left my father. She still owns it," she said, pointing to the single-wide mobile with the beige siding and forest green trim. "When Owen turned eighteen, he used the money he'd saved helping Mom with the Salty Dog to buy the one at the very end of the road, and after he and Sam bought their house on North Point, I bought it from him and moved out of our old trailer."

"Does your mom rent hers out? Or would she sell it?"

She glanced at him. "Why? You interested?"

"I might be." He flashed her a grin. "I want to move here, remember? And I can't stay in the cottage forever. Dad and Uncle Michael, and Christian and his wife use it, too."

She'd forgotten he was planning to look for a place of his own. She was so used to the idea of the St. Clouds staying in their North Point cottage two doors down from her brother that it was weird to think of Gideon living somewhere else in Sea Glass Cove.

"You'd want to live in a trailer?"

"Why not? It looks like your mom's done a fantastic job of maintaining it, and I like that it's sheltered by the trees."

"But aren't you a big shot photographer?"

"So?"

She didn't know how to explain the impression that he'd prefer a fancier house or the odd pleasure that came with the realization that he didn't, so she didn't try.

"Down the road, sure, I'd love to have a place like the cottage or like your brother's house, but for now, I just want to get moved here. And besides, something small like your mom's trailer would probably suit a bachelor better, anyhow. Less to clean and maintain."

"What about Liam?"

He frowned and stared up at the cedars and Douglas firs that towered over the mobile home village. Protected from the worst of the tree-stunting coastal winds by the ridges that wrapped around Sea Glass Cove, they stood far taller than the cedars that dotted North Point.

When he didn't answer, Erin said, "You'll get custody. You've got a great job with a steady income, and you're a great dad."

She didn't look at him again until she'd pulled into her carport and shut her car off, but she felt his gaze on her. At last, she turned to him, shifting her whole body toward him as much as she could still buckled in. Her pulse quickened.

"Thank you," he murmured.

The way he said it, with vulnerability and gratitude, reinforced what she'd felt last night—that he needed something from her. She'd needed people plenty of times in her life, but the only time someone had ever needed her, she hadn't been able to help. It was a strange sensation, and it tugged at her.

"You're welcome." She released her seatbelt. "Come on in."

She led him up to the tiny porch, unlocked the door, and stepped back to let him enter first, but he just stood there, frowning.

"You lock your door," he observed. "I didn't think anyone in Sea Glass Cove locked their doors."

"Habit." Since he apparently wasn't going to head in first, she stepped past him into the cool interior of her home. "Got into it when I lived in Santa Barbara, and I haven't managed to break it since I've been back."

"When did you live in Santa Barbara?"

"Moved there about four years ago. Stayed there for a year." She winced, unable to stop the memory of what had brought her to the renowned California city... and what had driven her back home to Sea Glass Cove with her heart shattered and her fear of relationships renewed. "Moved back right before Sam and Sean died—three days before, actually."

"What took you to Santa Barbara? Seems like quite a shift for a shy girl like you."

Erin chewed on the inside of her lip. This was *not* the kind of conversation she wanted to have on a perfect day like today, but she couldn't see any way to avoid the question, so she gave the shortest answer she could and hoped it would be enough. "Chaz."

Four

THE GRUDGING WAY she said it caught his attention, and he could guess who Chaz was without asking, but he did anyhow. "Who's Chaz?"

"My ex."

No surprise there. "Ah."

He wanted to press her about it, but now wasn't the time. It wouldn't be the time until she trusted him enough to open up about it, and getting to that point was going to take finesse and patience. Erin wasn't the kind to give up her secrets easily. He'd sensed that immediately, back in June, and he was beginning to suspect that once she did, he'd find a pure, compassionate heart well worth the wait.

"Let me show you around," she invited with unveiled relief in her voice.

The door from the carport opened into the wide living room, and he was surprised to see a newer wood stove sitting in the left corner. Sliding glass doors on the far wall opened onto a big deck.

Her double-wide mobile wasn't anything fancy, but with three bedrooms and two baths, it was plenty spacious. She told him that Owen and Sam had painted the wood-print paneling on the walls white and had installed the faux beams of weathered wood, but over the years since she'd bought it from them, she'd added her own touches—driftwood and shells and other nautical knickknacks and navy and aquamarine accents. The floor was covered with a speckled, neutral-toned carpet that invited him to kick off his shoes and curl his toes into its thick pile.

The kitchen had been remodeled in recent years, and he suspected that was Erin's doing. Hope had told him that Owen liked to cook, but the appliances were all fairly new—not quite old enough to have been installed when Owen and Sam had lived here. There was plenty of counter space without counting the snack bar that separated the kitchen from the living room. The dining room sat next to the kitchen on the same side of the house as the carport, and a walk-in pantry divided it from the living room. That *definitely* hadn't been part of the original floor plan. The wall on the living room side might've been, but not the pantry.

The whole place was artistically arranged and decorated, but rather than make him feel like he should be cautious so he didn't disturb anything, the soothing color scheme and personal touches invited him to sink into the couch's plush cushions and let go of his worries. It was a haven. Even the guest bathroom and rarely used spare bedrooms.

At last, they arrived at the room Gideon was most curious to see, though he wasn't about to admit *why* he wanted to see it.

"This is my favorite room," she said shyly, stepping aside so he could enter the master bedroom.

He wasn't disappointed.

A queen-sized canopy bed with a driftwood frame draped with filmy off-white and sea-foam green fabric dominated the room, drawing the gaze from the sliding glass doors that opened onto the back deck and the sunny hillside that was her back yard. She'd strung white-wired mini Christmas lights up the posts and along the canopy rails, and it was easy to imagine her curled up in bed with a book; those lights would provide plenty of illumination to read by. The quilt, which appeared to be handmade, incorporated all the colors and patterns of the sea.

Everything about her bed appealed to his artistic nature.

"This is gorgeous, Erin," he said, skimming his hands lightly over the driftwood frame. "Your whole house is."

"It was in pretty bad shape when Owen bought it, which is why he got it so cheap, but he did a great job fixing it up, and when Sam moved in with him…." She smiled fondly. "They're both artistic enough on their own, but the things they did together still amaze me."

He tilted his head. "You compliment their artistic tastes, but I daresay you have some pretty formidable talents yourself."

"Owen built this. And he helped me build the rest of it."

"Yes, but *you* guided him. Everything in here suits you too well to be anyone else's style. Even your brother's, similar as it may be."

She regarded him with eyes narrowed and lips pursed. "You're remarkably insightful."

He shrugged. "I've been trained by some top-notch professors and artists to analyze art and to find the artist's voice in it. Plus, it's my job as a photographer to read personalities. Gotta know how to get the exact expressions I need from my clients, right? That's what they hire me for."

"Makes sense." She tipped her head toward the sliding glass doors and started toward them. "Come on. I need to see what I have for fruit and veggies before we head to the store."

He started to ask why she was heading outside rather than to the kitchen, but as soon as he stepped outside, his question was answered. The hill he'd thought was a single slope was actually a narrow bowl, and dug into its south-facing slope was a gleaming subterranean greenhouse. Beside it, on terraces, were raised garden beds overflowing with vegetables. Awed, he followed Erin up the stairs to the greenhouse. The door opened into a small room filled with gardening tools—trowels and rakes, hoses, watering cans, empty pots, and everything else a gardener could possibly need. To the right was the door into the actual greenhouse, and he stepped into it close on her heels.

The air inside was warm and heavy with the earthy fragrance of growing things, and even with the top vents open wide to let some of the heat out, it was tropical. He paused at the top of the short staircase down into the greenhouse to take it all in. The entire south-facing wall was glass and angled to make the most of the winter sun. Currently, shade cloths were pulled across it. Built into the hillside with concrete walls on the east, north, and west sides, the set-up was remarkably efficient. Glancing up and shielding his eyes, he noted the grow lights installed along the beams between the panes of glass. The place was set up to grow year-round.

She had it all—small citrus and mango trees laden with fruit, melons, pineapples, and plants he had no hope of naming. She even had a dwarf coconut tree against the back wall, where the ceiling was highest. Various flowers added splashes of vibrant color, and his trigger finger twitched. What kind of photographer didn't have his camera with him in a place like this? This made twice in less than twenty-four hours that he hadn't brought it with him and twice he wished he had.

"You like mangos?" she asked.

"Love them."

"Here."

She plopped one on his upturned palm and handed him a small paring knife she kept in the greenhouse. As soon as he started peeling the skin away, the sweet fragrance of a perfectly ripe fruit curled around him, and he inhaled deeply. He sliced a chunk for her and one for himself, and when he sank his teeth into the soft flesh of the fruit, he purred. The juice trickled down his fingers, and he licked it away before it fell, unwilling to waste even a drop of its sweetness.

"This is amazing," he sighed. "Liam and my dad would *love* this place."

"You'll have to bring them over some day." She grabbed a basket of woven willow branches and made her way through her little paradise, perusing the offerings. "What are you in the mood for?"

"Something tropical, I think," Gideon replied, taking another bite of the mango. "I would've said whatever, but this mango spoiled me."

He offered to carry the basket for her and couldn't help but smile as she selected the fruits she wanted, absently pinching off a dying leaf here and there out of habit. When she was satisfied with the fruit harvest—more mangoes, a pineapple, and melons—they headed out to the garden, and she filled the basket with lettuces, tomatoes, sweet red, orange, and yellow bell peppers, an onion, radishes, a cucumber, and carrots.

"So… why do we need to go to the grocery store at all?" Gideon asked as they returned to the house and began the process of cleaning and preparing their harvest. "Because I'm pretty sure you have a wider variety of produce than they do."

"We still need meat, something to drink, and whatever other snacks," she replied. "You cook?"

"Only because I have to. I suck at it. But I think, if I had the set up you do, I'd find reasons to learn."

The smile she tossed him was exquisite—so open and honestly joyful. "I could teach you a few recipes while you're here. If you'd like."

"What? Today?"

"Not today. Owen usually does the campfire cooking. But sometime over the next few weeks."

Narrowing his eyes, he scanned her face. Was her invitation purely platonic… or did she realize what he wanted? When blush colored her cheeks and she averted her gaze with her smile turning shy, his heart leapt. The invitation might have friendly origins, but she was at least curious to see where it might lead. She was holding another door open for him and waiting to see if he'd step through this one, too.

He glanced around her home. He felt he'd been invited to take a glimpse into her soul, and if her home was a genuine representation of her spirit, she was possibly the most beautiful woman he'd ever met.

Now might be a terrible time to test the waters of a new relationship, but if he didn't jump in with her, she might not make the offer again, and there was too much potential to ignore. He'd just need to be careful with her.

Turning back to her, he smiled. "I'd love that."

Five

GIDEON IDLY TAPPED his fingers against the lens cap of his camera and watched Erin, Daphne, and Hope put the finishing touches on their elaborate two-room driftwood fort. His trigger finger itched, but he hesitated. It was impossible to capture everything that soaked his senses; even the best shot would fall short.

At his feet, his black Lab sprawled with her ears back, tongue lolling, and eyes gleaming with the pure joy of having exhausted herself swimming and fetching. He reached down to ruffle Shadow's ears and murmured, "Happy dog."

She tipped her head back and regarded him with a grin of agreement.

Owen strode over from the cooler with what was

left of the pineapple from Erin's greenhouse and joined him on the log. Gideon took a piece, popped it in his mouth, and nodded his head in thanks.

"Man, that's amazing," he groaned. He reached for another piece, wiggling his brows at Owen and saying with a practiced lisp, "You sexy beast, you always know just what I like."

His companion's shoulders shook with silent laughter. "It's good to hear you joking around again. You had me worried last night."

"You and me both." Gideon ate the last chunk of pineapple and leaned back with his forearms resting on the log behind him; it made a decent if not horribly comfortable backrest. "That greenhouse of Erin's is something else."

"Isn't it? When she asked me to help her build it, I had no idea how incredible it would be."

"Why am I not surprised it was her idea?"

"She's pretty amazing," Owen agreed. "I wish she'd let more people see that."

Gideon nodded, adding that piece of information to his rapidly growing file of Erin-related thoughts. It fit right in next to the impression he had of her—that she was highly introverted and amazingly complex—and the suspicion that she was the exact opposite of Hannah. Sad as it might be, he agreed with what his father had said to him after he'd asked Hannah to leave. If he wanted to be happy, he needed a woman as different from Hannah as he could find.

He shifted his gaze out to the cove where Owen's mother and her beau were currently engaged in an all-out splash fight in the kayaks. The vibrant joy and affection on their faces…. Maybe that was something he could capture. He nudged Owen. "Think they'd mind if I took a few pictures of them?"

"Probably not. And in fact, if you get a good one, I'll pay you for it. Mom's birthday is coming up pretty quick."

"You've got a deal." Where he was sitting was as good a vantage as anywhere else, so he snapped a few shots of Red and Andra. Then he settled his camera in his lap again. "That's about the most adorable thing I've ever seen."

Owen's lips lifted in a fond smile. "They're great together."

"Wish my dad would give it another shot. I'd love to see him smile like that again."

"Maybe he will." Owen leaned back, stretched his feet out in front of him, and knitted his hands behind his head. "It's hard to come back from a loss like that."

"You would know better than most," Gideon remarked. "But it can be done."

"Yes, it can."

His gaze wandered back to the girls' fort, which appeared to be finished. Hope and Daphne were now poking through the line of driftwood piled at the base of the sand dunes for treasures, and Erin sat on the big log in front of her construction.

"Owen, can I ask you a question?"

"Sure."

"What is it with your sister and those forts? She built one when Liam and I were out for the solstice, too."

"That's a holdover from when we were kids, before we moved to Sea Glass Cove. Whenever Dad started yelling and pushing mom around, I'd take Erin down to the beach and build forts with her. Promised her she was safe there, that I'd never let anything happen to her."

Gideon's brows rose. Whatever answer he'd been expecting, that wasn't it. He lowered his gaze to the sand beneath his feet and shoved some into a pile with his toes before he spoke, trying and failing to swallow the sudden guilt for doing exactly what he'd promised himself he wouldn't—asking her brother for the keys to her secrets. "That's deep."

His companion only nodded.

"Your dad was a genuine SOB, I take it."

"Yeah, he was."

Frowning thoughtfully, Gideon turned his gaze back to Erin. Sitting there on the log in front of her fort with the golden evening sunlight aglow on her face and in her long hair, she made every bit as beautiful an image as the one she'd made last night perched on the railing of her brother's deck. Innocent contentment softened her features, and he had no trouble picturing her as a young girl huddled in another fort on another beach, sheltered as much by her big brother's protective arms as by the sea-worn driftwood.

Giving Gideon's shoulder a brief squeeze, Owen stood and strode over to his sister's fort. When he sat beside her and tucked his arm around her waist, she laid her head on his shoulder. He said something to her, and by the warmth in their smiles and the direction of their attention—out to the cove—Gideon didn't need to hear the words to know what the man had said.

If he was careful and if Owen kept Erin adequately distracted, he might be able to sneak around and get a better angle. With the light, he didn't want to be right in front of them, but a forty-five-degree angle would be exquisite. And with the sharp contrast bringing out the textures…? A shiver of excitement trickled through him. He slipped from his seat and made his way slowly toward a spot that would give him the ideal angle. Just as he reached it, crouching so he was level with them, Erin tilted her face toward her brother, her expression one of pure contentment. It was a look Gideon suspected she reserved only for Owen. To say she adored her brother was a vast understatement; the love she had for him was the paragon of unconditional, and given their history, it was no wonder.

Suddenly, a potent desire to earn such affection

from her stole the breath from him.

He pressed the shutter button with awe and giddiness pulsating through him in alternating waves. *That* was the shot—the kind he lived for as a photographer. The kind that captured emotion in its purest, most honest light. Without checking, he knew the shot would be stunning in every sense of the word.

He sat back on his heel and lowered his camera, and the movement caught Erin's eye. For a moment that would be forever burned into his memory, he was bathed in the warmth of her fondness.

Then it was gone, replaced by a veil of a smile that—while it still held a modicum of fondness for him—was cool by comparison. That's why he hadn't wanted her to know he was photographing her. He never would've gotten a shot like the one he knew was stored on his camera's memory card.

Come back to me, he thought, lifting his camera.

But the magic was gone, and after another dozen shots of Erin and Owen gazing straight into the lens, Gideon switched his camera off and rose to his feet. When he turned to head back to the campfire and his camera bag, his heart nearly fell out of his chest. Red's elder son, Ethan, stood a few paces away with his arms folded loosely and a grin lifting one corner of his mouth.

"I hope you got that shot right before Erin realized you were there."

"I did."

"Hope tells us you're a photographer by trade and not just a hobbyist."

"That's right."

"Dad didn't want to bring it up tonight—no business at beach parties—but are you, uh, looking to pick up a job or two while you're here? Or is this strictly a vacation?"

"It's a vacation, but since I'm looking to move here, I'm not going to turn down any jobs that come my way. What do you need?"

"Dad'd like some new photos of the campground to revamp the website and marketing materials. By a professional, this time. Is that something you could squeeze in?"

"Sure."

"And Liz over at the Tidewater Inn needs a photographer for some events they have coming up this month. The guy who was supposed to do them was in a motorcycle wreck last week, and he's in pretty rough shape. Won't be back to work for at *least* a few weeks."

Gideon winced. "I'm sorry to hear that. I hate taking a guy's work when he's down."

"Yeah, it sucks, but if it isn't you, it'll be someone else. I talked to Liz when Hope said you'd be coming out for a month, and she was excited to work with you again. I didn't know you took those shots in the lobby until she told me. They're gorgeous."

"Thanks. Yeah, I took those years ago—before I graduated from college. Dad's the one who sold them to her." Gideon smiled. "That was actually what made me think I could make a living with my photography. Tell Liz to give me a call at the cottage—the number's the same. And I'll stop by the Grand Dunes tomorrow, see what you boys need."

"I'll pass it on. Thanks, Gideon."

"Anytime."

He left to help his father and Andra pull the kayaks out of the water, and Gideon chuckled when Red smiled in his direction and then turned a scowl on his son. From where he stood several yards away, Gideon plainly saw Red's mouth form the words *I thought I told you no business tonight.*

Tilting his head, he narrowed his eyes. Huh. He'd been back in Sea Glass Cove less than twenty-four hours, and he already had a couple jobs lined up. One might say that was a sign that moving here would be good for him.

Now if he could just get this whole custody debacle settled and get Liam out here with him… life would be just about perfect.

Unbidden, his gaze slid to Erin only to find her sauntering toward him looking oh-so-sexy with her sun-gilded hair roughened by the soft sea breeze. It was tempting—*so* tempting—to reach for her hand and pull her into his side. The desire to be the object of her affection lingered, and it was potent.

"That was a sneaky thing you did back there."

"Sneaky, maybe, but I'll bet you dinner I got a shot of you and Owen that your mother is going to adore for the rest of her life."

"And how long until we find out who wins such a wager?"

"Your mom's birthday. When's that?"

"August thirteenth, so a week and a half."

Before he could say he didn't want to wait that long to see how the bet would play out, she changed the subject.

"Gorgeous evening, isn't it?" she asked.

"Mmm. It is."

He tipped his head to the side and studied her. She'd caught her bottom lip between her teeth, and her eyes sparkled like she wanted something but was too shy to ask for it. She stared down the beach at her mother and Red, but her eyes weren't following them as they maneuvered the kayaks back into the water. Apparently they'd only come in to grab refreshments.

"I think it's about time to break out my guitar," Gideon announced.

"That would be lovely," Erin murmured, still watching the couple in the kayaks. "Since it appears no one else is going to get another turn."

"Doesn't bother me. They're enjoying themselves, and that's a wonderful thing to see."

Laughing softly, she turned toward the parking area and, without invitation, fell into step beside him. He made no mention of it. Would she notice?

She strolled quietly with him along the trail through the sand dunes all the way to the parking area. When they reached the sand-dusted blacktop, he slowed his pace.

"Erin?"

"Hmm?"

"What if I don't want to wait a week and a half to take you to dinner?"

She stopped abruptly and her eyes rounded. "What do you mean?"

"I'd like to take you on a date."

"Like a *date* date?"

"Yes, a *date* date. I told you, you intrigue me. You have such depth to you that I can't help but want to dive in."

"I hope you're talking figuratively, because I don't do sex on the first date."

He stared blankly at her for a moment. Where had that come? Then he laughed. "I didn't mean it like that. I wasn't even thinking—"

Laughter sparkled in her eyes and curved her lips into an impish smile. "That's obvious."

"Forget it. You're evil," Gideon teased. "I should keep my pure soul far from your wicked charms."

She snorted. "Pure soul? Ha!"

"All right, so I'm not so pure."

The mirth slowly left her gaze, and he almost reached out to her as if he could somehow catch it as it drifted away.

"All joking aside…." She lowered her gaze to the pavement and rose up on her toes, then sank down. "It's probably better to be up front with you. I don't do relationships."

"You don't do them… or they're difficult for you?"

"The first," she replied slowly, "because of the second."

"I figured as much."

She met his gaze and held it, probing, waiting for him to explain how he'd guessed that. He wasn't going to spoil the evening by telling her how he'd arrived at the conclusion. The dark memories Owen had shared with him weren't for gorgeous evenings like this.

"So, how about that date?"

"You still want one? Even though it probably won't go anywhere."

"I do. Now even more than before. But I don't want you to say yes because you feel pressured into it. I want you to say yes because you want to."

She chewed on her bottom lip as the battle between deep-rooted habits, curiosity, and what Gideon hoped was eagerness played out across her face. Finally, she sighed and smiled, and he grinned in response. She wanted to say yes.

"Don't look so smug about it," she quipped, "but yes. A date with you sounds fun."

"Fantastic. And for the record, this isn't my smug face. This is my delighted face."

"Ah. Good to know. When?"

"Would tomorrow be too soon?"

"Not at all."

Much to his astonishment, she slipped her hand into his and gave it a tug. They walked to his SUV like that, and with his free hand, he dug his keys out of his pocket and hit the button twice to unlock all the doors. He didn't want to let go of her to fetch his guitar from the back seat, but reluctantly, he did.

As he opened the case, lifted the glossy maple instrument out, and slipped the strap over his shoulder, he frowned. He'd forgotten to grab his phone when he'd left the Salty Dog with Erin.

"Hang on a second," he said, and reached for the passenger-side door.

He found his cell phone right where he'd left it in the glove compartment.

"Hey, there's a rule about those, you know," Erin teased. "No cell phones allowed at beach parties."

"I know, I just need to…."

His voice trailed off when he glanced at the lock screen and saw that he'd missed eight calls. Crap. One was from Hope, another was from his father, and the rest were all from Hannah and all within the last hour. Double crap.

"I have to call her back," he said, unlocking the phone. He didn't bother listening to any of Hannah's voicemails. She never called that many times in a row unless something had happened to Liam.

"Call who back?"

"Hannah. She called six times." He swore under his breath. The phone rang and rang, and panic surged as one scenario after another raced through his mind, each more horrific than the last. Liam had fallen off the swings at the park and re-broken his arm. He'd snuck into the kitchen and cut himself trying to make himself a sandwich because Hannah had been too lazy to make him one. He'd been hit by a car playing out in front of Hannah's sister's house. Nausea churned. "Please God, let him be all right."

"You think something happened to Liam?"

"Why else would she have called so many—"

"It's about time you call me back," Hannah snapped from the other end of the line. "I've been calling you for *hours*."

One hour, a tiny voice corrected in the back of his mind even as adrenaline lanced through him at the sound of her voice. "Please tell me Liam's okay. What happened? Is he hurt? How bad is it?"

"He's fine. Nothing happened," she retorted. "But you need to come get him."

It was almost a minute before her words sunk into his brain. *He's okay. He's not hurt.*

He barely had time to let out a sigh of relief before anger ignited. "You scared the hell out of me, Hannah!"

Twenty-four hours. He'd barely been here for a full rotation of the world and she already wanted to get rid of her son. The timing smacked of spite, and his scowl deepened. He should make her keep him, but he wouldn't do that to their son.

"Please come get me, Dad!" he heard Liam yell in the background. "I don't want to stay here anymore. Please."

The tears in his son's voice was a spear of ice straight to his heart. "Put Liam on the phone please."

"When are you coming?"

"I'll leave first thing in the morning. Put him on the phone, Hannah."

"No. You can talk to him when you get here."

The boy's scream of outrage was cut off as the line went dead, and Gideon stood rooted in place, paralyzed by the urge to hurl his phone to the ground. A slender hand slid the device from his grip. He raised his gaze from his empty hand, and the concern in Erin's sea-green eyes sliced through his anger, sweet and soothing. Shyly, she slipped her arms around him, and he sank back, leaning against his car as he tucked his arms around her waist and dropped his head onto her shoulder. Quivering with fury and a potent need to let her quiet strength bolster him, he sighed.

"Looks like we'll have to reschedule our date. I'm sorry."

"He's okay, though, right?" Erin murmured. "She wants you to come get him?"

He nodded.

"You said she's at her sister's in San Francisco?"

Again, he nodded.

"That's an eighteen-hour drive."

"I know it is." Even to his ears, his voice sounded weary.

"Would Hannah meet you in Mendocino?"

"I doubt it." He lifted his head, frowning. What an oddly specific question. "Why do you ask?"

"Well… Owen and I have a cousin there, and he was planning to take some more items down for her to sell in her shop, but…."

Her lips curved slowly, shyly, catching his attention.

"Maybe I could go in his place so he can stay home with Hope and Daphne. Then you and I could split the driving, and if you don't mind sleeping on the couch, we could stay at Lauren's and save money on hotel rooms. I was thinking of volunteering, anyhow, but now…."

"I can't ask you to do that."

"You aren't asking. I'm offering."

"In that case…." The last of his frustration came out in a rush, and as it left him, he was able to smile. "That would be wonderful. Thank you."

"Crisis averted?" she asked.

"For now."

"Then let's get back to the party, shall we?"

Six

ERIN PARKED GIDEON'S CAR beside Lauren's in the
driveway around the back of her cousin's place, shut it
down, and almost groaned in relief. What a day. A drive
that should've taken them twelve hours had taken almost sixteen thanks to an over-turned logging truck that
had backed traffic up for miles. They'd left at six this
morning after loading the car with Owen's creations
with the hope they'd make it in time for dinner. Instead,
it was now nearly ten.

"We're here," she sighed.

When Gideon didn't answer, she glanced over at
him and let out a huff of laughter. He was out cold, and
with sleep erasing the frown that had furrowed his
brows frequently in the hours since his less-than-cordial

phone call with his ex, he was beautiful. She hesitated to wake him, unwilling to bring him back to realm of the conscious where all his troubles waited.

Yawning, she gave in and nudged him. "Gideon. We're here."

"Already?"

"Don't you mean *finally*?"

"Yeah. Finally. That's what I meant," he mumbled. He stretched with a groan, sat up, and scrubbed his hands over his face. "Thanks for driving the rest of the way. I was done."

"Obviously."

When he turned tired eyes and a lopsided smile on her, her heart fluttered. For a moment, she held his gaze, enthralled. She couldn't look away if she'd wanted to. Then a blossoming of light in the dark night caught her attention, and she glanced toward her cousin's deck. The open door spilled light onto her porch, and the woman herself strode to the top of the steps, clad in plaid fleece pajama pants, a plain black tank top, and a broad, welcoming grin. Erin climbed out of the car and jogged up the stairs to hug her cousin.

"It's so good to see you!" Lauren said, squeezing the breath out of Erin. "Where's your gentleman friend? Ah, there he is."

She let out a low whistle and nudged Erin playfully with her elbow. Erin's face heated uncomfortably, and she hoped Gideon was too far away to notice the teasing. He was heading toward the porch with both his overnight bag and hers clutched in his hands, and if he'd caught the exchange, he gave no indication.

"I was going to grab mine in a minute," she said.

Despite the weariness that made his eyes and shoulders droop, he offered her a lopsided grin. "You're welcome."

"Thank you," she replied quickly. "Lauren, this is Gideon St. Cloud, Hope's cousin. Gideon, this gorgeous woman is my cousin, best friend, and one-time college roommate, Lauren King."

"It's a pleasure to meet you, Lauren," Gideon said, cresting the stairs. He shifted Erin's bag to his other hand and shook Lauren's offered hand.

"I do believe the pleasure will be mine if the rumors are true," Lauren quipped.

"What rumors?" Erin asked, whirling on her cousin.

"Owen might've mentioned seeing a few sparks between you and this fine-looking gentleman here."

"I'm gonna kill him," Erin muttered.

"No, you won't," Gideon remarked. "You love him too much."

"Doesn't mean I won't maim him."

"Anyhow," Lauren interrupted, tipping her head toward her door. "Come on in. I saved you both a plate of dinner if you're hungry, and if not... I've already got the couch and the spare bed made up for you."

"You're a goddess," Gideon said with a sound that was half groan of relief and half purr of pleasure. "Thank you for your hospitality. Especially considering the short notice."

"I'm glad I could help. Sorry it didn't work out so you could get your boy tonight."

"Yeah. Me, too." He set the bags on the floor beside the island separating Lauren's kitchen from the living room and rolled his shoulders when he straightened. Then he yawned—the kind of deep yawn that made his eyes water. "I need to call Hannah."

"Why don't you do that while I heat up your enchiladas. They're nothing fancy, but they're homemade and hearty."

"That would be wonderful. Thank you."

"Call her tomorrow," Erin said gently. Then she grinned. "Or text her and don't reply tonight."

Gideon pointed at her as he turned toward the door. "That's genius."

Erin followed him outside, leaning against the post of the porch roof as he trotted out to the car to retrieve his phone. By the time he returned with the text already sent and the phone set to Do Not Disturb, Erin was fighting to restrain her laughter.

As soon as he noticed her expression, his lips twisted in chagrin. "Find me amusing?"

"Highly. That's the second time *today* you've left your phone in the car, and it's only the second time we've been out of it longer than it takes to fill the tank. Plus, you left it in your car all day yesterday."

"I hate cell phones," he retorted. "If I didn't need the thing for work, I probably wouldn't have one. What?"

Erin's face and sides ached from holding the laugh in. "You're cute. I know where Liam gets it."

The way his expression shifted from amusement to despair added a fresh crack to her heart beside the dozen others this day had put there. She bit her lip and cursed herself for opening her mouth. When he sat heavily on the stairs and buried his hands in his hair as he propped his elbows on his knees, she sat beside him and slid her hand across his back. After a moment, he turned his head toward her.

"I know I've said it at least two dozen times today," he murmured, "but thank you for coming with me. It's stupid to feel so wrung out over picking my son up, but I am."

"If it were just picking him up, you wouldn't be. It's the driving all the way to Sea Glass Cove from California, having one day to recuperate before turning around and driving another twelve hours... all because Hannah is being a vindictive harpy."

He snorted. "True that."

"Let's go back inside. I bet Lauren has those enchiladas ready for us. And then you should probably get to bed before you fall over. You want the spare bedroom or the couch?"

"Couch is fine, but thanks for offering the room. I've already impositioned you enough."

"Um, Gideon?"

"Hmm?"

"I'm not sure 'impositioned' is a word."

He snorted. "It should be."

She rose to her feet first and offered him a hand up. He took it, and a groan escaped him as he stood. As she'd predicted, Lauren had two plates sitting on the island, two steaming enchiladas on each with two glasses of mint-garnished ice water.

"This is a fantastic place you have here," Gideon remarked after he'd finished eating. He carried his plate, fork, and glass to the sink, washed them, and set them in the strainer before turning toward Lauren, who regarded him with brows raised and her lips curved in a disbelieving smile. "That area under the loft—that's your gallery, isn't it?"

"Yes, sir, it is."

"And the house is an addition?"

"Right again. I had it built shortly after I bought the gallery."

"Well, your artistry shows. It's beautiful."

Erin glanced around the space with a new appreciation for her cousin's home. It *was* beautiful—a mixture of nautical and urban grunge with a dash of country charm that shouldn't work together but did. What had been the exterior rear wall of Lauren's gallery was now an interior wall, but rather than cover the brick, she'd left it exposed. She'd had the roof of the gallery removed and a "loft" built over the store, and it now held two decent-sized bedrooms and a full bathroom. The open walkway was bordered by a wrought-iron railing. The high-ceilinged living room was decorated similarly to Erin's own home with a lot of weathered wood, shells, thick mooring ropes, and antique nautical items including an anchor, portholes, and cleats. Where Erin preferred shades of blue-green from pale sea foam to deep teals, Lauren preferred bolder colors—rich navy blue and sassy red trimmed in gold.

"I was wondering if Erin's and Owen's artistic talents came from the McKinney side or the King side, but looking at your home, I'm guessing it comes mostly from the King line."

"Unfortunately, yes," Erin muttered. "I thought you were tired."

"I am exhausted. So, if you ladies will excuse me…."

"I should probably get ready for bed, too," Erin sighed.

While Gideon vanished into the bathroom beneath the stairs up to the loft to prepare for bed, she carried her bag up to the spare bedroom. She changed into her pajamas and took a moment to freshen up before she headed down to the kitchen. She perched on one of the stools at the island. Lauren asked if she'd like a glass of iced tea, and even though it meant she'd probably have to pee in the middle of the night, she nodded.

She was just stirring honey into it when Gideon reappeared. His hair was down—she hadn't seen it like that yet—but raked back from his face. Clad in modest burgundy and white plaid pajama pants and a plain white T-shirt just tight enough to give a hint of the toned chest and shoulders beneath, he was distractingly sexy. A peculiar sensation quivered deep in her core, a primal reaction she hadn't felt in a long, long time... if ever. At this precise moment, she couldn't recall ever feeling it for Chaz, though she must have.

She caught Lauren's raised-brow look from the corner of her gaze and shifted her attention to her cousin. Lauren set another glass of ice water garnished with a sprig of mint in front of Gideon and he dipped his head in thanks before he took a long drink.

Quit staring, Erin commanded herself.

It didn't work, but thankfully, he was too tired to notice.

"Good night, ladies. Lauren, thank you again."

"You're welcome. We'll try not to keep you up with our gossiping. It's been a while since we've had a chance to sit down together and catch up face-to-face."

"Phone calls just aren't enough sometimes," he added. His lips quirked briefly. "Don't worry about disturbing me. I don't think an air-raid siren could keep me awake at this point."

"Good night, Gideon," Erin said.

He hooked her hand with a finger, brought it to his lips, and pressed a kiss to her knuckles, holding her gaze the entire time. The gleam in his eyes wasn't what she would call desirous. More... reverent. And definitely grateful. "Good night, *bonita*."

She didn't watch him walk away, but as soon as she heard him adjusting the blankets and getting comfortable on the couch behind her, she turned her head toward him.

Lauren turned off the kitchen lights and nodded her head to the pair of recliners sitting perpendicular to the couch. As they made their way into the living room, they turned off the rest of the lights, leaving only the dim glow from the bedrooms in the loft to illuminate the house.

"How are things in Sea Glass Cove?" Lauren asked conversationally, keeping her voice low. "That new waiter of yours pull his head out of his rear yet?"

"He was close to an hour late yesterday, but he volunteered to take my shifts today and tomorrow without question. And Mom said he showed up early today, so I hope he has."

Erin tried and failed to keep her gaze from Gideon. He started out with his back to the room and his face to the back cushions of the couch, but that didn't last long. He rolled onto his other side, and shortly after, slumber slackened the graceful lines of his face.

It was incredible how sleep could ease the worries from a person and leave only the beauty of him to be seen.

"How's everything else up your way?" Lauren inquired.

"Wonderful. Hope and Daphne are back, so Owen's been walking around with this big dopey grin plastered to his face. Mom and Red send their love... and Ethan says hi."

Lauren rolled her eyes. "Didn't he just get engaged? Again?"

"Yes, and I don't think this one's going to work out, either."

"Not if he's asking you say to hi to another woman."

"I'm thinking the trouble is this other woman."

"Well, he'd best make it work with this newest fiancée because it's never going to happen with me. How's everything else? Business at the Salty Dog still booming?"

"As always. You can cut the small talk," Erin murmured, still gazing at Gideon. "He's asleep. Has been most of the time we've been chatting."

Lauren's relief came out in a rush, and Erin braced herself. "All right, spill it. What's going on here?"

"I'm just helping a friend and my brother."

"Uh-huh. I don't buy it. Not with the way he

looks at you. Or the way you're looking at him right now. And you don't drive twelve hours with a man you've known less than a week to get his son. Some people might do that, but not you."

"I don't know what's going on," Erin admitted. "And I think that may be for the best. I like him, and I think he likes me, and maybe if I don't know what's going on, I won't be able to overthink it and ruin it."

"Oh, he *definitely* likes you." Lauren reached over and gripped her hand. A tender smile softened her expression. "All teasing aside, this is a good thing you're doing."

Erin nodded. In some ways, Lauren was right. Gideon certainly seemed glad to have her along, but that might change tomorrow when he had to face Hannah. Erin was the reason he hadn't gone all the way to San Francisco, and discounting *that*, who knew what Hannah would think about Gideon contemplating a relationship with another woman.

"Yeah, we'll see," she said.

"Hey. It'll be fine." Lauren released her hand and stood with a yawn. "I know you and I always joke about how we don't do relationships, but I don't think that truly fits you. So… I hope this works out for you. He seems like a great guy."

"I thought Chaz was a great guy, too, remember? I even ditched my mom and the Salty Dog to move to Santa Barbara to be with him."

"Yes, you did, but Gideon isn't Chaz. Look at how long he stayed with his child's mother. I assume, from what Owen told me, it was only because he thought it was what his son needed. Can you see Chaz putting anyone before himself for that long?"

Erin shook her head, but didn't comment on what Chaz would or wouldn't have done in Gideon's situation. It was just as painful to imagine him being too selfish to put his child first as it was to picture him suffering through a broken relationship to do what was best for his kid. "He broke up with her because he finally realized it *wasn't* what was best for Liam. Or, at least, that's what Owen said Gideon told him."

"You believe it?"

Her eyes again sought Gideon's sleeping form. "Yeah, I do."

"Well, then. I don't think a man like that could ever do to you what Chaz did. Granted, we both know how little I know about men."

"Once burned, twice shy." Erin let out a sniff of laughter. "Heaven help the world if you ever find a man willing, able, and worthy to heal your burns because you'll set the whole thing on fire."

"Never gonna happen." Lauren yawned again. "I need to call it a night. Gotta get up early to find homes for Owen's stuff. G'night, cuz."

"Good night."

Erin sat in the chair a few minutes longer, frowning in Gideon's direction and tapping her fingertips against her chin. Abruptly, she stood and followed Lauren upstairs. She had a lot to consider, but what she'd said to Lauren about not knowing and about her tendency to overthink everything was true. So she wasn't going to think about any of what they'd talked about or what the morrow would bring. She was going to go to bed and leave tomorrow's worries for tomorrow.

Easier said than done.

Seven

ERIN TURNED THE BACON and glanced at the clock on Lauren's microwave. It was half past nine, but Gideon was still snoozing away on the couch. Hungry and bored waiting for him to wake up, she'd started breakfast. That was now nearly finished. She chewed on her lip. Should she rouse him now or wait for him to wake up when he was ready? On the one hand, he'd be more rested for their drive home, but on the other, he was anxious to see his son. Would he be upset with her if she let him sleep a little longer?

Idly, she wondered if he'd be less serious and more like the lighthearted man she'd met in June once Liam was back in his care. If someone were to ask her right then which she preferred, she'd have no answer.

She enjoyed his jesting, but the moments of vulnerability endeared him to her, made her feel connected to him. Would that disappear if, when he had his son back, he reverted to the wise-cracking flirt?

It didn't matter what *she* wanted. That's not why she'd offered to come. She'd come to support him because, on such short notice, who else would? His father was hours away in the Puget Sound area, and Hope was in the middle of a pretty big life change right now, and as wonderful as that was, it left her with a shortage of energy to expend on her cousin. And while he could undoubtedly handle this on his own, Erin didn't want him to. Sometimes it was nice to have someone to lean on, like she'd leaned on her brother most of their lives.

Yeah, we're gonna go with that story.

It was easier than admitting how eager she'd been to spend more time with him.

Hearing the crunch of gravel under tires, she glanced out the kitchen window but saw nothing, so she turned back to the stove and pulled the bacon off the heat and lined a plate with paper towels. Everything else was ready, so in a couple minutes, she'd have no excuse not to wake Gideon.

A demanding knock sounded on the door and she nearly dropped the tongs and the bacon. She quickly laid the rest of the slices on the paper towels so they didn't continue cooking and trotted across the dining room to the door. She glanced at the couch. Gideon showed signs of stirring, but the loud knocking hadn't brought him to full consciousness yet, and she scowled in irritation at whoever was pounding on the door. Who would be knocking at *this* door rather than going straight to Lauren's shop? Anyone who knew her would know she was there, and anyone who didn't would likely be here on business… and they'd go to the shop anyhow.

A woman gorgeous enough to be a star of runways and fashion magazine covers stood on Lauren's porch.

"Can I help you?" Erin greeted as cheerfully as she could manage.

The woman looked her up and down with a brow lifted. "You're Lauren King?"

"No, I'm her cousin, Erin McKinney. Lauren's in her shop. It's around front, if you—"

"McKinney? Owen's sister?"

Hannah. Of course.

Somehow, Erin wasn't surprised. And yet… she was. Dressed in a manner somewhat contradictory to her beauty in fitted black sweatpants and a lightweight red zip-up hoody over a scoop-necked tank top with her silky dark hair messily tossed by the sea breeze, this tall, amber-eyed goddess was not at all the kind of woman Erin could picture Gideon with. He struck her as the kind who preferred lower-maintenance women. God, that sounded harsh, especially considering she knew

nothing about this woman but what he had told her...
and his opinion wasn't exactly objective. Still, high
maintenance was Erin's instinctive impression. Harsh or
not.

"You must be Hannah," she replied. She craned
her head to look behind the woman. "Where's Liam?"

"Waiting in the car. I wasn't sure this was the
right place. Where's Gideon?"

"He's still asleep."

"Correction," Gideon remarked from the living
room. "I *was* asleep."

Erin winced and turned toward him. He sat on
the couch with his hair a mess and his head turned toward the door but not far enough to look at her or his
ex. After a moment, he raked his hair back from his face
and pushed off the couch. He still looked exhausted.

"What are you doing here, Hannah?" he asked
tiredly as he joined Erin. "I said I'd call when I was up."

"It's almost ten o'clock."

"So?"

"*So...* I was supposed to drive back to the city last
night."

"Maybe you should've waited to go to your sister's until *after* I returned from San Diego and picked
Liam up. Then *neither* of us would've had to make this
trip."

Erin cleared her throat, and Gideon and Hannah
jerked their heads toward her. "Should I get Liam and

help him put his bags in your car, Gideon?" She turned to Hannah. "I've made bacon, eggs, and pancakes, if he's hungry."

"We had breakfast," the younger woman retorted.

"Don't be rude," Gideon snapped. He reached for Erin's hand and gave it a quick squeeze—a clearer statement of boundaries to Hannah than his words. "Thank you, Erin. That would be great."

When he dipped his head to kiss her cheek, her breath sucked through her teeth. If taking her hand was a statement of boundaries, *that* gesture was an even clearer declaration of what she was to him. And Hannah caught the meaning. Her eyes rounded, but she recovered quickly, snapping her mouth closed and replying with a haughty smirk.

Erin slipped past her outside and was surprised when Gideon followed her out and closed the door behind himself. Another line drawn. Lauren wouldn't have minded him inviting Hannah in to talk, but Erin doubted he would even if he were at the cottage in Sea Glass Cove rather than a guest in someone else's home.

As she strode out to Hannah's car, she heard the woman snarl at Gideon, "Who is she to question me about *my* son?"

"Someone who cares enough about *our* son to think of his needs," he snapped. "And she wasn't questioning you, just asking. It's a little thing called common courtesy, Hannah. Something I see you still have no concept of."

Erin lengthened her stride, anxious to be out of hearing before their argument escalated further. It wasn't any of her business, but she couldn't stop herself from pondering her inclusion in it. Not with the ghost of a kiss on her cheek. Had that been just for Hannah's benefit, to retaliate for her spitefully inconveniencing him? Or was there more to it? He certainly hadn't been shy about his interest in Erin. On the one hand, she didn't like being used as ammunition against his ex, but on the other… it was nice to hear him tout her virtues.

Hannah's car was a newer Toyota Camry, and Erin wondered—unfairly, perhaps—if she or Gideon had bought it. Shaking her head, she glanced in the back seat, but Liam wasn't in it. Instead, she found the little boy strapped into the front seat playing with a teddy bear that had seen better days. The tawny fur was matted and lackluster from too much love and too many washes. She hesitated, noting the boy's frown and the way he tugged at a thread attaching the bear's button nose. Poor guy. This had to be as hard on him as it was on his parents.

Finally, she tapped gently on the window and opened the door after he saw her. His frown disappeared and a smile blossomed in its place.

"Hey, Liam," she greeted, leaning in the door. "Remember me?"

He nodded vigorously. "Yeah. Hi, Erin."

She tipped her head to his bear. "Who's your friend? I don't remember meeting him when I met you earlier this summer."

"This is Oliver. I forgot him at Mom's last time."

"Well, hello, Oliver." She shook the bear's small paw. "It's a pleasure to meet you."

Liam laughed quietly, but after a moment, his amusement faded. "Where are my mom and dad?"

"They're discussing a few things."

The rest of his smile disappeared completely, and an even deeper frown returned. "Fighting, you mean."

Erin caught her lip between her teeth and sighed. There didn't seem to be any point in lying to him. "Yes, fighting. Hey, I know your mom already fed you breakfast, but might I tempt you with some pancakes? Or bacon and eggs?"

He nodded. "I'm hungry. We ate hours ago. Mom woke me up at seven, and all we had for breakfast were the snacks left over from the trip yesterday."

"In that case, come with me. We'll go in through my cousin's store so your parents can have some privacy while they talk. How much did you bring with you? Maybe we should put your stuff in your dad's car first."

"I have just Oliver and my backpack."

Just a backpack? Hopefully Gideon had thought to bring a few more things with him to the cottage for his son.

To keep Liam's mind off what his parents might

be fighting about, Erin quizzed him about his trip yesterday and what he and his mom had done in their time in San Francisco as they stowed his backpack in Gideon's car and headed around to Lauren's gallery. It was more difficult than she expected to keep him talking; it didn't sound like he and his mom had done anything kid-friendly in the city. Mostly, he'd just sat around playing by himself while she visited with her sister, who seemed to have little patience for him.

"She didn't take you down to Fisherman's Wharf or Hyde St. Pier to see the ships? What about the aquarium? Those were my favorite parts of the city when Mom took Owen and me when we were kids."

Liam shook his head. "Dad took me there last summer, and I wanted to go back, but Mom didn't want to. She said it was too crowded and too much money."

"I'm sorry to hear that, little man. Are you excited to spend a month in Sea Glass Cove with your dad?"

He nodded, but the frown was still in place.

She held the door of Lauren's gallery open for him, and once it closed behind them, she squatted in front of him. "Hey. It'll be okay. I know it doesn't seem like it now, but they'll work this out."

His eyes rounded and tears gathered along his lower lids, and he shook his head slowly, pinching his lips together.

"Yes, they will. You know how I know?"

He nodded.

"Because your dad loves you." She reached for his hands and gave them a squeeze and was stunned when he yanked them away to throw them around her neck. With only half a second's hesitation—did he really just say his mother didn't love him, or was she hearing things?—she folded her arms around him. "Your mom does, too, even if she doesn't always know how to show it."

Sensing someone's gaze, she lifted her head. Lauren approached with a strange gleam in her eyes. Alongside curiosity and concern were memories, and Erin winced. She hadn't considered how having Gideon and Hannah battling over their son under her roof might affect her cousin.

"Everything okay?" Lauren asked.

"He's having a tough morning," Erin murmured. "Gideon and Hannah are out back arguing, so I thought it'd be better to bring him through this way. I hope you don't mind."

"Not at all. Am I smelling bacon?"

"Yeah. You hungry?"

"I could eat again."

"Liam, would you help me bring Lauren her second breakfast?"

"Second breakfast?" he asked. With a sniff, he straightened and wiped his eyes and his nose with his sleeves. "Like hobbits eat?"

Erin laughed softly. "Yep, just like hobbits eat.

Come on, kiddo."

She ushered Liam toward the door between Lauren's gallery and home and caught her cousin watching her with a faint, contemplative smile.

What? Erin mouthed.

Lauren shook her head. "Nothing. Just seeing a new side of you. Guess we'll find out if your man is smart enough to see it, too."

My man? Erin shook her head and strode into the house without responding.

It was an appealing idea, calling Gideon hers, but….

Catching sight of him through the window in the door out to Lauren's porch—he was still fighting with Hannah—she stopped herself. As she took in the anguish and guilt twisting his beautiful features, the need to protect him from it clenched around her insides. She flexed her fingers at her sides, fighting to keep her hands from curling into fists, and commanded herself to stay out of it. It wasn't her business.

Then she made the mistake of glancing down at Liam. His eyes were trained on his parents, and there were tears in them again.

Screw it.

She fixed Liam a plate of food first, nodded in acknowledgment when he quietly but politely thanked her, then marched toward the door.

Because there was no *but*. The idea of calling Gideon *and* his son hers had taken root, and if they were hers, it was her right to defend them both.

Eight

AS SOON AS THE WORDS were out of his mouth, Gideon regretted them. Erin had done an incredibly generous thing for him, and dragging her into this mess with Hannah was a crappy way to repay her. It didn't matter that Hannah had brought her into it first with that snippy comment; he should've defended Erin and left it at that, not used her to insult his ex.

Stupid. But *stupid* summed up much of his relationship with his son's mother.

"That came out harsher than I intended," he admitted. "I'm not awake yet, and yeah, I'm pissed I had to turn around and drive to Mendocino only a day after I drove to Sea Glass Cove. Did you honestly expect me to jump when you snapped your fingers and be happy about it?"

Hannah didn't respond, only glared at him.

"Let's just get Liam's things moved from your car to mine so I can see my son and you can be on your way back to your sister's. Just please tell me you remembered to bring Oliver this time."

"Yes, we brought the stupid bear."

That *stupid bear* had been a gift from Gideon's father, something he'd bought for his stillborn daughter and held onto for twenty-some years to give to his first grandchild. There were few material things in this world Gideon would walk through fire to save, but that stuffed bear was one of them. He'd fetch it even before his camera equipment and computers, and he made his living with those.

With a growl, he swallowed the urge to call her every fowl name he'd ever heard of in English *and* in Spanish and glanced toward his car just in time to see Erin toss Liam's backpack into the back seat. When they headed around front to her cousin's shop instead of returning to Hannah's car for the rest of the boy's things, Gideon frowned.

"That's it?" He turned back to his ex. "Just his backpack?"

"That's all you sent him with."

"Oh, for Christ's sake, Hannah! I sent him with two duffle bags, too. Where are the rest of his clothes and his toys?"

"I guess they're back home."

"That's all you took to San Francisco for him?"

"That's all I had."

"What about the clothes he has at your apartment? Didn't you bring any of *them*?"

"He's outgrown everything."

He swore under his breath and scrubbed his hands over his face. For almost a minute, he stared beyond her at the ocean with his teeth clenched. When he leveled his gaze on her, she scowled. Why had he ever thought she was beautiful? He'd never be able to un-see the irresponsibility and immature vindictiveness, and it tainted even her undeniable physical appeal.

At last, he said, "I don't get it."

"Don't get what?" she asked distractedly, scowling after Erin.

"I don't get why you're fighting me for custody when you clearly only want to be a parent when it suits you."

"I love my son."

Gideon snorted.

She whirled on him. "Do you really think so little of me?"

"You don't want me to answer that. His arm hasn't been out of the cast long enough yet."

"Hey, you're the one who bought him that stupid trampoline."

"Yeah, and I always sit out there with him while

he jumps on it to make sure he's being safe! I sure don't let him jump onto it from the swing set. What were you doing instead of watching him? Texting on your phone like the day he and Sean McKinney wandered down to Hidden Beach by themselves?"

"You're never going to let that one go, are you? Jesus, it's been three years, Gideon!"

"I'd've let it go a long time ago if it were a one-time slip. But it wasn't. How many times have I had to stop in the middle of a photo shoot to pick him up from school because you forgot it was your day to get him? How many times have I had to drop what I was doing to clean his cuts and scrapes because you couldn't be bothered to take care of him? You want to know why he comes to me when he's hurt or scared, Hannah? Because he knows I'll be there!"

That struck a nerve. She snapped her mouth shut and glared at him. The seconds ticked by, and the shine of tears in her eyes cooled his anger a few degrees.

"That's not fair. You're good at this whole parent thing. I don't know what I'm doing."

"And you seem to have no desire to learn. I have no idea what I'm doing most of the time, either, but I do what needs to be done."

"Is the plan still for you to bring him back this weekend?" she asked, her voice wavering.

He didn't have time to analyze her evasive change of topic before his mouth fell open. "You've got to be kidding."

"No, I'm not. Why would I be?"

"Well, you sure were in quite a hurry to get rid of him."

"Regardless of what you think of me, I *do* love my son."

Her chin wobbled and tears welled in her eyes, and he winced as he watched her fight to contain it. He didn't like seeing her cry. He couldn't say he'd ever truly loved her, but he cared enough for her that the doubt that the tears were even real hurt him. She'd pulled so many tricks in the months since he'd asked her to leave that he couldn't help but wonder if this was just another tug on the leash to remind him she still held the other end.

"I haven't seen my son in two weeks," he said quietly. "I'm not going to turn around and bring him back in a few days, but I'll bring him back the weekend after next."

"That'll have to be good enough, I guess."

He was mildly surprised she wasn't going to argue with him about *that*, too. "Let me ask Erin to send Liam out so you can say goodbye to him and get on the road. I know you're anxious to get back to your sister's."

He started toward the door, but when his hand landed on the knob, her voice stopped him.

"Who is she?"

"Erin? She's Owen McKinney's sister."

"No. I mean… who is she *to you?*"

"That isn't any of your business."

"Actually, it *is*. I have a right to know what kind of woman you're bringing around our son. Especially when he hasn't shut up about her."

Sighing, he said, "She's a friend."

"I don't believe you."

He ground his teeth at the indignant air she affected. "Fine. She's a friend I hope will become more."

"Become more…."

Liam wasn't the reason she was asking, merely a cover for something else. She'd been out with at least two men since they'd broken up, so it couldn't be jealousy… could it? No, not quite. The way she watched him with the facade of parental righteousness giving way quickly to insecurity—she chewed on the inside of her cheek, something she did when she was trying to keep a grip on her emotions until she could escape a situation—was closer to regret than jealousy.

Abruptly, he straightened, catching himself; he was leaning toward her, ready to be there for her when she reached for him. He folded his arms across his chest again. "All you need to know about Erin is that she's great with Liam. Otherwise, leave her out of this. Because you have no room to talk after you brought that prick Cal around."

"And you're Mr. Perfect who's never made a mistake."

He started to say that his mistakes had cost him seven years of his life, but Erin's voice cut him off.

"Excuse me, but there's a little boy inside who's upset because his parents are too busy fighting to even notice him."

Her words were polite enough, but her tone was sharp, and he whipped toward her.

"You need to set your differences aside until he isn't watching."

Fire flashed in Hannah's golden eyes, but to Erin's credit, she held the younger woman's gaze with her back straight and her jaw set. Even with fury still swirling through him like a restless tide, he was awestruck by the power in her. Hannah's expression turned black, and Gideon stepped between them before she could act on the venom seething in her veins.

Hannah snarled. "How dare you—"

"Is this really how you want him to see you?" Erin asked. She shifted her gaze to Gideon. "For God's sake, you haven't even said hello to him yet."

Guilt and anger boiled together in a poisonous stew, but then he noticed the way she held his gaze, unflinchingly with the faintest hint of tenderness. Oh, she was *smart*. With one seemingly caustic rebuke, she'd momentarily placed herself in opposition to him, which put her on Hannah's side by default, and it had the desired effect. His ex's lips twitched into a haughty smile, her anger at Erin expertly diffused.

Abruptly, he left them on the porch and went into the house. Liam leapt off the stool at the kitchen island and raced across the dining area. As Gideon wrapped the little boy in his arms and inhaled the familiar scent of him, he sighed, trembling with relief. God, he'd missed the little bugger. How could he have let Hannah get under his skin like that?

"I'm sorry, bud," he murmured. "So sorry. I shouldn't have fought with your mom. I should've come straight in here to be with you."

"It's okay," Liam whispered.

"No, it's not. I don't care how angry or hurt I am. You are the only thing that matters."

"I don't want you to be angry. Or hurt."

Gideon exhaled. "This won't last forever. Your mom and I will find a way to work through this. Thank goodness Erin was here, huh?"

"Yeah. She makes yummy pancakes."

He gave a sniff of laughter. "I bet she does. Come on. We need to say goodbye to your mom."

Unwilling to let go of his son, he carried the little boy outside. Erin tried to slip past him into the house, but he snagged her hand and whispered, "Thank you."

She dipped her head in acknowledgment without meeting his gaze and escaped inside as soon as he released her hand.

Hannah waited exactly where he'd left her, and at last, he lowered Liam to the porch so he could give his mother a hug goodbye. The little boy didn't move toward her, instead clinging to Gideon's side. Hannah's brows dipped briefly.

"Go give your mother a hug so she can get on the road."

He shook his head, and hurt brightened Hannah's eyes.

"Go," Gideon said quietly but firmly. "You don't want her to remember this for two weeks, do you? She'll be so sad."

"I don't want to go with her in two weeks," Liam said defiantly, glaring at his mother.

Hannah jerked back and her eyes sprang wide.

"Liam!" Gideon chided, but it was too late.

Hannah was already turning away with tears spilling over. Gideon called after her, but she ignored him. She jogged out to her car, yanked the driver's side door open, and sank into it. As she sped away, spraying gravel as she went, he let out a growl and swore under his breath.

"Well, that's that, I guess," he sighed.

He gripped his son's hand and led him back inside. Erin had finished the dishes and was sitting at the island with a plate of eggs, bacon, and pancakes sitting untouched in front of her. When she heard them approaching, she looked up. The apprehension that widened her eyes sharply contrasted the unyielding strength he'd seen only minutes ago, and he paused.

"I'm sorry," she murmured.

"For what?" he asked, letting go of his son's hand and striding to her. He took her hand and drew her to his feet, then wrapped her tightly in his arms. After only the tiniest hesitation, she melted into his embrace. "I needed that."

"I guess you aren't mad at me for overstepping my bounds."

Her voice was adorably muffled against his neck, and he let out a sigh that was half relief and half affection. And did his best to ignore the way her warm breath on the curve of his neck and the weight of her head on his shoulder made his pulse lunge.

"You said and did exactly the right things." He sighed. "I have to stop fighting with her—it only hurts us more. Especially Liam."

He leaned back with her arms still hooked around him and clasped her face gently in his hands, skimming his thumbs over her cheeks. He expected her to look away, but she held his gaze, and a soothing calm washed over him.

"You're incredible," he murmured.

"I don't know about that."

He tucked her hair behind her ears, consumed by the shy desire hazing her eyes. "I do."

A guttural sound from his son drew his attention, and he laughed at Liam's curled lip.

"Are you two gonna kiss?" the boy asked around

a mouthful of scrambled eggs.

"Not yet," Gideon replied, but he dipped his head to kiss Erin's cheek. Finally, he released her and grabbed the empty plate she'd left on the counter for him. "Did you tell her thank you for breakfast?"

"He did," she replied. "So... I've been meaning to ask. Does this trip count as our first date?"

"I'll let you decide that." He lowered his voice so Liam couldn't hear. "But either way, I'd still like to take you out to dinner when we get home. I can ask Hope to watch Liam for a few hours. I'm sure he and Daph would love—"

She shook her head, and he snapped his mouth closed, confused.

"This trip is all I get?" He turned his gaze back to his plate. Just a few moments ago, he'd seen desire in her eyes, and there had been only the briefest moment of reluctance in her arms when he'd hugged her. Had that been no more than the support of a loyal friend? His shoulders droop. "I don't blame you. Maybe I was wrong to think I'm ready to start dating again. Obviously, I need to fix a few things with Hannah first, get to a point that I don't want to scream at her every time I have to deal with her."

"I agree with that second part, but I wasn't saying no to another date. You can't leave Liam alone right now. We can find something to do to include him."

He kissed her hard on the lips, clasping her face

and drawing her off her stool toward him. When he let her go, she stared at him in wide-eyed shock edged in wonder, and he couldn't remember anyone ever looking so beautiful. The shy innocence that turned her pupils into deep pools rimmed by the slimmest ring of sea green sucked him in.

"Thank you," he breathed.

"Um… you're welcome?"

"I thought you said you weren't gonna kiss," Liam muttered, stabbing another bite of pancake.

Erin laughed softly. "Apparently he changed his mind."

The shyness in her voice drew her to him, and he leaned closer, asking permission to kiss her again. God, he wanted to kiss her. When she didn't lean away, he touched his lips lightly to hers and angled his body against hers. She slipped her arms around his neck, responding to his coaxing with breathtaking curiosity. He skimmed his tongue over her bottom lip as instinct and desire filled his head with cotton and buzzing that made conscious thought impossible.

She tensed, sending needles of ice through the haze of passion, but they weren't strong enough to distract him. With that faintest taste of her spurring his hunger, he needed more. He took her face in his hands and deepened the kiss, slipping his tongue between her lips.

The spell shattered.

Erin jerked back, and the desire in her eyes vanished quickly as something darker widened them. Abruptly, she turned away, snatched her half-eaten breakfast, and took her plate to the sink.

He stared at her back, shaking. His heart hammered, but it wasn't desire that made it pound. It was adrenaline, triggered by a primal reaction to the shadow in her eyes.

What had just happened?

As shock gave way to disappointment, his shoulders sagged as a weight descended on him and threatened to crush him to the floor. He sidled around the island and joined her at the sink, cautiously touching her shoulder with his fingertips. She flinched.

"Erin?"

She shook her head, pinching her lips between her teeth. Craning his neck so he could get a better look at her face, he frowned. She looked like she was trying not to cry.

"What did I do?" he entreated.

"Nothing," she whispered. "I'm sorry, I…."

"No. *I'm* sorry," he murmured. "I didn't mean—"

"It's not you, Gideon. It's not what you did."

"Then what is it?"

Again she shook her head and offered him a forced smile that only deepened his confusion. Whatever it was that shadowed her eyes, she wasn't going to be able to talk about right now. He lowered his head to kiss her shoulder, and this time she didn't wince, but she also didn't give any indication that she wanted him to continue. Discouraged and with his head spinning, he returned to his stool at the island, but he wasn't hungry anymore.

"Way to go, Dad," Liam muttered.

Gideon ruffled his son's hair and gave him the brightest, most teasing smile he could manage. "I'm not doing so great with women this morning, am I."

"Nope."

"Finish your breakfast. We need to get on the road."

All throughout the rest of their meal and packing for the ride home, Erin was her usual warm and cheerful self, and Gideon ached to ask her about what had happened, but the occasional wariness and regret that flashed in her eyes when he got too close made him hesitate.

Once everything was loaded in his SUV, they stepped into Lauren's gallery.

"You sure you don't want to stay another night?" the woman asked.

"Positive," Gideon replied. "We need to swing through Beaverton on the way back to Sea Glass Cove to pick up some more of Liam's things. I brought some, but I was expecting him to come back with the clothes and toys I sent him to his mother's with."

"Pity. Well, come back any time."

"Thank you, again, for your hospitality, Lauren. It was a pleasure meeting you."

"Likewise."

He took Liam out to his car and buckled him into his booster seat in the back seat while Erin said her farewells to her cousin. When she returned, he leaned against the hood and held his hands out to her. She hesitated, but then she took them and allowed him to pull her into his arms, and he folded them around her with a sigh of relief.

"Tell me not to worry about what happened in there," he said gently, "and I'll keep my questions to myself until you're ready to answer them."

"Don't worry about what happened in there," she replied. "For now, anyhow."

"That's not going to make me worry less."

"I told you relationships are hard for me. But I'm trying. Is that enough for now?"

"I guess it'll have to be. I *am* sorry, for whatever I did."

She flashed him a grateful smile. "It wasn't you. But thank you."

He brushed his lips across her cheeks, further relieved when she didn't flinch or pull away. Finally, he released her and forced his lips into a grin he didn't feel. "Let's get this show on the road. I don't know about you, but I'm ready to get back to Sea Glass Cove to relax."

They climbed into his car, and as he drove north out of Mendocino toward home, he knew it was going to be impossible not to worry about Erin's reaction to his kiss, despite his promise that he wouldn't.

The longer he thought about it, the more he believed it wasn't a lack of chemistry. For someone who claimed to shun relationships, she had opened herself to the possibility of one with him with remarkable ease and willingness. Everything about the way she interacted with him was encouraging—she was warm and witty, sweet and steady—and no matter how many times he ran it through his head, he saw no red flags to make him think she was faking any of it.

Except….

That shadow in her eyes when she'd pulled away, and his visceral reaction to it. Where had *that* come from? Because he knew with a gut certainty it didn't stem from disgust or dissatisfaction.

It was born of fear.

Nine

"I'M GLAD TO HEAR you and Gideon and Liam are going to dinner at your brother's," Andra remarked. "Guess that means you're not still avoiding the poor man."

Erin winced as she dropped her order pad on the counter with the rest and slipped her pen into the cup beside it.

She didn't like avoiding Gideon, and she hadn't set out to do it intentionally. Their ride home from Mendocino had been pleasant enough, like he hadn't kissed her and she hadn't jerked away from him. But she hadn't seen much of him since they'd gotten home at almost three in the morning on Thursday. He and Liam had lazed around the cottage that morning, and then she'd worked the evening shift at the Salty Dog. And she'd taken double shifts the last two days with the excuse that she wanted to make up her lost wages. She doubted he believed that, and her mother *certainly* didn't. She couldn't explain why, but she just... couldn't face him yet. Not even yesterday, when he'd brought her a gorgeous bouquet of white tulips and hyacinths—a creative apology fitting for an artist like Gideon, even though he had nothing to apologize for. Of course, he didn't know that, and she hadn't been able to drum up the courage to tell him why.

"You have been," Andra continued when she didn't respond. "What I can't figure out is why."

"I'm sure you can guess."

"He's not Chaz."

"I know he's not."

"Do you? Do you *really* know that? Because you're not acting like you believe it. Chaz was a go-with-the-wind artist. Gideon may be an artist, too, but he's grounded. Someone like Chaz wouldn't be fighting so hard for custody of his son."

"Lauren said the same thing."

"And he definitely wouldn't have been able to build the solid business your beau has on his own. You and I both know Chaz's brother is the only reason their brewery is flourishing."

Erin nodded, but couldn't find her voice to say all those points—as reasonable as they were—wouldn't mean anything if she couldn't get past the gag reflex every time a man kissed her.

"It's unfair to judge him by what Chaz did," her mother continued. "If I'd've judged Red by what your father did, I would've pushed a good man away, and I wouldn't have found the love of my life."

Erin's brows furrowed. She knew her mother meant well, and her choice of anecdote was certainly a valid one; Red *was* a good man, and Erin held him almost highly as she held her brother. But her mother didn't have the same deep-seated, crippling issues Erin did—issues she knew firsthand could suck the life out of a relationship.

"You need to tell him, my girl. Give him the chance to show you if it matters to him."

Again, she only nodded.

"All right. If you don't, I will. He's been too polite so far to ask, but—"

"You'd really interfere in my love life?" Erin eyed her mother warily. The determination burning in her mother's eyes made her squirm. She'd interfere, all right—without hesitation. "Why?"

"Despite what you have tried so hard for so long to convince yourself of, marriage and family suits you, and I think, if you were willing to look deep in your heart, it's what you want. I want my girl to be happy."

"Thanks, Mom."

"Get out of here. Go get prettied up for your

dinner date tonight. I know you hate makeup, but sometimes it can give a woman a boost of confidence, and I suspect you need that right now."

With a soft laugh, Erin gave her mother a quick peck on the cheek and headed out of the Salty Dog. She didn't head home to get "prettied up," though. Instead, she pulled into the northern beach access parking area.

The fort she'd built Gideon's second evening back in Sea Glass Cove was mostly intact, and she took a few minutes to repair it. Then she sat on the log in front of it, sheltered from the glaring midday sun by the fort, and let her gaze wander from the waves breaking restlessly on the beach to the distant horizon hazed by an off-shore fog bank. Tendrils of clouds reached toward the coast, and the air was thick and heavy—the summer's stifling heat was breaking, at last.

Sighing, she glanced over her shoulder into her fort. A soothing calm washed over her. Here, in the cool shade filled with the briny scents of the sand and sea, she was safe. She had no clear memories of the events that had once driven her and Owen to the driftwood piles back in Eureka, California, but she remembered his words and the cocoon of safety the walls of their forts had imbibed from them as if he'd whispered them in her ear only moments ago.

Nothing bad will ever happen to you here. I'll keep you safe. I promise.

No ten-year-old boy should ever need to promise

his six-year-old sister those things.

Of course, no promise—however deeply held—could erase the damage.

Erin hugged herself. She didn't like thinking like this, didn't like admitting there existed a darkness her big brother couldn't chase away.

That was why she'd been avoiding Gideon for the last three days. Her reaction to his kiss was irrefutable proof that she couldn't be fixed. Certain gestures and touches would always trigger her, would always make her jerk away even from a man who made her want to try them.

She was going to have to find the courage to tell him, and probably today, because her mother wasn't bluffing. She didn't know what timeframe Andra was operating on, but she *would* tell Gideon the uncomfortable reason why Erin struggled with relationships, and the thought of her mother revealing such intimate details of her psyche mortified her.

Anxiety exploded, stabbing the muscles all along her spine with needles of burning acid. Her heart raced, and she forced herself to take a long, deep breath to slow it. Then she pushed to her feet.

"I thought I might find you here."

She flinched at the sound of his voice as a new rush of anxiety-fueled adrenaline flooded her veins. Good God, she hadn't been this jumpy since that go-dawful day Chaz had revealed just how little he cared about *her* needs. She chewed on her lip, took a few more deep, measured breaths, and willed herself to be calm.

Ready or not, he was here.

"Gideon," she breathed.

"Hi." He stopped a dozen paces away and shoved his hands in his pockets. "I stopped by the Salty Dog, but Andra said you'd already gone home. When you weren't there, either…."

She slipped her smartphone out of her pants pocket and held it up. "You could've saved yourself all that driving with a simple phone call or a text."

"Left my phone at the cottage."

"You really do hate that thing, don't you."

With a sniff of laughter, he stepped closer. "Mind if I join you?"

Rather than answer with words—she wasn't wholly certain she could keep her voice steady—she resumed her seat on the log and patted the spot beside her. For a long time, they sat in silence, watching the waves. It was so tempting to rest her head on his shoulder and curl her fingers around his arm… and that was something she'd never felt the urge to do with Chaz. At least, not so strongly and not after those first few weeks early in their relationship.

Deciding it couldn't do any more harm than bolting on him after he'd kissed her, she gave in and was rewarded when he rested his head on top of hers and let out a sigh like this was exactly what he needed.

"Where's Liam? And Shadow?"

"Up helping Owen and Hope and Daph prep dinner. I wanted—needed—some time alone to talk to you."

He let that hang, perhaps waiting for her to respond, perhaps trying to find the right words to express whatever it was he needed to say. If he was waiting on her…. She had no idea what to say or where to begin. Or what she wanted from him, for that matter.

"What happened in Mendocino?" he asked at last.

"I freaked," she answered. "Obviously."

"I get that. But why? What did I do wrong?"

"You didn't do anything wrong, Gideon. I'm just…." She stopped herself short of saying *broken*. He wouldn't believe that. And she didn't honestly believe it herself. She was *damaged*, yes, but not broken.

"Do you want me to slow down?"

Her brows furrowed. "No… because slowing down won't help."

"What will? Whatever you need from me, I'll do it. But I can't if I don't know what you need."

She snorted. "I need to have had a different start to my life."

"Owen said your dad was a real piece of garbage. He also said that's why you build these forts—because you and he used to build them to get away from him."

Oh, Owen. Her lips curved, and love for her brother was a warm glow in the gloom. Once again, he was there, protecting her and making things easier. *Thank you.*

"But there's more to the story than even Owen knows. More than I knew until three years ago when my boyfriend and I broke up."

"That was Chaz?"

She nodded. "He needed the kind of physical attention I wouldn't give him. He said *wouldn't*, but the truth is, I *couldn't*."

"Please tell me this isn't going where I think it is," Gideon said, his voice strangled.

Erin looked up at him. The color had leeched from his face, and the muscle in his jaw worked. Sensing her gaze, he lowered his eyes from the horizon to her face. She'd been where he was right now—trying to make sense of a despicable act. First was the shock. Then the disbelief. Then the anger and the despair. Finally, the relief because she had an answer to the question of why even the raging hormones of adolescence hadn't kick-started the ravenous sex drive so many of her friends had been swept away by. An explanation for why physical intimacy was a source of anxiety rather than the pleasure it should be.

"I was molested as a child," she confirmed. Even though she'd had three years to assimilate that information into her sense of being, it still made her feel dirty and exposed to say it out loud. She ignored those feelings and pressed on. "No, it wasn't my father—at least not that Mom knows. It was his buddy. The night we left, Mom came home to find Dad drunk and passed out on the couch while his friend had me pinned in the recliner with his hands under my dress."

"Oh, God...." Gideon jerked upright and stared down at her, his face ashen. "Jesus, you were *six*!"

"Yep."

"Who could...?" He shook his head. "I'll never be able to answer that, so I'm not even going to try."

"I tried to find an answer. For a while. But there isn't one. And I'm not sure if that makes it easier or harder."

They sat in silence for almost a minute before he spoke again.

"I'm not sure I *want* to know, but I have to." He swallowed and held her gaze as more seconds ticked by. His beautiful dark eyes were apologetic. "Was that the only time... or were there others?"

"I don't know, but Mom is pretty sure there were others. A few years later, he was convicted of raping his two stepdaughters, so, yeah, it seems likely that it wasn't an isolated incident."

"You don't remember?"

"No. As impossible as it seems, I don't remember any of it. I honestly don't. The only memories I have of back then are vague ones of my parents screaming and breaking things. The only clear ones are of Owen and me building our forts. But I always felt like something

126

was wrong with me." She snorted. "The boys in high school called me a prude."

"Why did your mom wait so long to tell you?"

He didn't say it accusingly. He was only asking a question to give himself a better picture of what had happened. She appreciated that.

"She didn't want to remind me of it, hoping that would be the end of it. Obviously she was wrong because I can't even French kiss a guy I really, really like without wanting to gag. After Chaz and I broke up— *why* we broke up—well, she realized not knowing was only hurting me more."

"I'm sorry, Erin."

"Why? You didn't know. And I thought maybe… just maybe…. But no. Not even with you."

"That sounds like a compliment—not even with me," he murmured. "Like you wanted it to work."

"I *did* want it to work." A fragment of abalone shell caught her eyes, gleaming amidst the duller debris the tide had washed against the driftwood. She fiddled with it for almost a minute before she spoke again. "I wanted it to work with Chaz, too, in the beginning. But every time he said something like 'if you just tried a little harder', that only made it worse. I tried to suck it up and just do it because he needed that physical connection, but the more he tried to make me enjoy it, the less I could stand to let him touch me."

"I don't mean to be insensitive, but you aren't

a...."

"Virgin? No. Chaz was my one and only, though. He thought the problem was my inexperience, but nope. Clinical sexual dysfunction." She sniffed and twisted her head toward Gideon. "How's that for too much information?"

"Well, considering that I'm interested in a serious relationship with you, I don't think there's such a thing as too much information. I'm flattered that you trust me enough to tell me all this, to be honest. What made you break it off with him?"

"A couple months before the end, things changed. It was like he flipped a switch. Suddenly, he was in a great mood all the time again, and he stopped asking for sex. He even stopped trying to kiss me."

Her eyes stung at the memory, so she pinched them closed. *I will not cry.*

"He was cheating on you," Gideon surmised when she didn't continue.

The disgust in his voice was a heady dose of validation for her bruised heart, and she almost smiled.

"I couldn't give him what he needed, so... he found it with one of the waitresses at his brewery. When I realized the reason for the change, I confronted him and he didn't even try to deny it. In fact, he, uh, suggested his affair was good for our relationship because I was off the hook for sex."

"You're serious? He actually said that?"

She nodded. Tears welled in her eyes, making the world waver, and she cursed them, hugging herself tightly. When Gideon's arms came around her, she leaned into him, grateful for his gentle support as the tears spilled down her cheeks.

"I've had three years to get over it," she said, sniffing. "And I'm over him... but I don't think I'll ever get over what he said. What if I'm never able to fully enjoy sex or even kissing? How can I expect a man to love me when I can't be everything he needs?"

"Oh, *querida*," Gideon whispered. "The right man will love you no matter what because he'll know that intimacy and sex aren't the same thing and that there are a million ways to be intimate. What we're doing right now, for example."

"That's easy to say, but—"

"Erin."

He slid his hand under her jaw and tipped her face toward his. Tenderly, he brushed the tears from her cheeks. Then, lowering his head, he pressed his lips to hers in a gentle kiss.

"I'm old enough and wise enough to know what I want and what I need from my partner, and so far, you have it all."

It took her a few moments after he released her before she could open her eyes. Then she met his hopeful gaze and smiled. "That was nice."

"So that kind of kiss is okay?"

She nodded.

"Good to know. Be patient with me, though, all right? I'll try not to push you, but some habits and instincts have deep roots, and I'm likely to slip. A lot, at first."

"Be patient with *you*? Shouldn't it be the other way around?"

He shook his head. "No. I take you as you are, which means I'm the one who needs to learn where your limits are. I think we can both agree that's where Chaz screwed up."

She tucked her arms around his ribs and buried her face against his chest, pinching her eyes closed. How could she feel like she was being crushed beneath the weight of ineptitude while simultaneously feeling so light and free with gratitude that she feared she might float away if she didn't have Gideon to anchor her to the log?

"In Chaz's defense, he didn't know."

"That shouldn't have mattered. He should've cared enough to see it wasn't something you could help. He should've...." He let the words trail off, and after a moment, he cleared his throat. "Doesn't matter now. His loss is my gain. But do me a favor, will you?"

"Um... okay. What?"

"Don't ever take the blame for his actions again. He chose to cheat because he's a dick. That's it."

She didn't agree with him, not yet, but the conviction in his voice made her want to, and she suspected he would convince her if she gave him enough time.

"Thank you," she murmured. "For that, for listening… for just being you."

"That may be the first time I've ever been thanked for being myself."

Her face warmed with a faint smile. "That's a shame."

"Isn't it? All right, *querida*, now that we've had this deeply serious heart-to-heart, how about we have a little fun and crash a dinner party?"

Laughing, she let him pull her to her feet. Impulsively, she threw her arms around his neck. "Thank you."

"What for this time?" he asked, folding his arms around her.

I could stay right here forever. Sighing as contentment eased the heartache, anger, and grief, she leaned back in his arms. "For making me laugh when I shouldn't be able to."

He chuckled at her words. "Glad I can return the favor." He kissed the top of her head. "Come on."

With her arm around his waist and his around her shoulders, they walked to the parking area.

She had no idea if this would last or if Gideon would really be able to settle for a woman who couldn't be as physical as he might like, but in this moment, she couldn't understand why she'd avoided him for the last three days. Talking to him had been so easy, and with an instinctual certainty, she understood that she wouldn't have been able to lay herself so bare like that with Chaz. He'd never given her the sense of emotional safety Gideon had in such a short time, and the difference between the two men gave her hope.

Ten

GIDEON NEARLY DROPPED the potted orchid when Erin opened the door at his knock. Dressed in a flirty ivory sundress that showed off her graceful neck and shoulders, she was absolutely breathtaking. She'd left a few tendrils of hair to frame her face and pulled the rest back in a braid. When she ducked her head with her cheeks pinkening beneath his gaze, he saw she'd tucked a pale blue silk flower into the top of it that matched the five teardrops of blue topaz that glittered on the delicate silver chain around her neck.

Since she never wore makeup, the tiny bit of eye shadow and mascara she'd applied tonight caught his attention. It was an understated effect, but it drew attention to her eyes... those incredible eyes the color of the sunlit sea frothing against the cliffs, so full of innocence and shy desire.

"Wow," he breathed. "You look amazing."

"You didn't say what we were doing for our date, so I tried to find something that would work for anything."

"I...." He swallowed and tried again. "It's perfect."

She caught her bottom lip between her teeth, and her eyes sparkled with his praise. "You look pretty amazing yourself."

He glanced down at his khaki slacks and crisp white button-up shirt. He'd thought leaving the top couple of buttons undone would be a good idea—casual with just a hint of formality —but he now felt completely underdressed even though his attire matched hers well. Because his words wouldn't cooperate, he simply thanked her and held the orchid out to her.

"It's beautiful. Thank you." She laughed softly. "Flowers on Friday and now an orchid. You're going to spoil me."

"You deserve to be spoiled."

She stepped aside, inviting him in, and he followed her into the dining room, touched when she set the orchid in the center of her table and stood back for a moment to admire it. He wasn't sure she'd appreciate it, but when he'd spotted it in the local florist shop, it had reminded him of his parents' first meeting.

"There's a story behind this," Erin remarked. "An orchid is an unusual gift, isn't it?"

"I suppose to most people it is."

"But not to you."

His lips twitched. "No, not to me. My dad grows orchids… because my mother did and because that's how they met. He was working in the grocery store in a small town, covering for the gal who managed the florist department, and he couldn't for the life of him figure out why this one orchid was dying. My mother happened by and told him what was wrong. Two weeks later, he proposed with that same orchid. Tied a ring to its stem."

"What a beautiful story. Your dad sounds like a very sweet man—a true romantic." She turned to him and slipped her arms around his neck, then pressed a feather-light kiss to his lips.

"He is."

"His son seems to have inherited a lot of that from him."

"Until I met you, I was beginning to think I hadn't inherited much at all."

"Mmm. Spoken like a true romantic." She leaned back with her arms still hooked around his neck. "Two weeks, though? Seriously?"

"Seriously." Gideon chuckled. "They were meant for each other, and they were wise enough to see it. Come on. We're going to be late for the only part of our date I actually have a schedule for."

"Are you going to tell me what you have planned?"

"A picnic dinner on the beach courtesy of the Tidewater Inn. And I'm going to apologize in advance for any interruptions. Liam is out kayaking the cove with Hope and your brother, and it's possible they'll pull in to shore to say hi."

"There's nothing to apologize for. I told you we shouldn't exclude him. Remember?"

"I do. And if I didn't know he'll have way more fun in the kayaks, I'd feel guilty." He dipped his head to kiss her neck. "But this is something I need to do for you and you alone."

"I don't ever want you to set your son aside for me, Gideon."

"I believe that. And if I didn't, we wouldn't be having this conversation."

Taking her hand, he led her outside. He couldn't let her continue down that line of thought because their conversation on Sunday had awakened thoughts and emotions he hadn't yet had time to organize, and he was in danger of letting some of them slip. She wasn't ready to hear any of it yet, and he wasn't sure if it was a temporary gut reaction or something far more lasting. This was their first real date, after all—not counting the trip to Mendocino. How could he possibly know if she was the one already?

Dad knew. He knew when Mom helped him save that or-chid.

One memory preoccupied his mind all the way from the Forest Haven Mobile Village through town to Tidewater Point—their beach party on the summer solstice, the day he'd met Erin. Glancing at his date and noting the faint smile that graced her features as she gazed out the windows, he remembered the moment she'd finally let go of her cool reserve. It had come right as she and Liam had put the finishing touch on the driftwood fort and erupted in gleeful celebration. He'd gotten his first real glimpse of the beautiful, vibrant spirit she protected from the world, and he'd realized with a clarity that still awed him that maybe his father's stories of falling in love with Maria at first meeting weren't exaggerated. In eight years, Hannah hadn't once shown him anything like it, and in that moment watching Erin and his son, he'd seen a glimpse of the kind of life he wanted.

The next day, he'd called his lawyer to start the process of filing for full custody of Liam.

They'd reached the Tidewater Inn, so he put those thoughts on hold. He held her door open for her and offered a hand to help her out of the car. With her hand hooked around his elbow, they walked into the inn and were greeted by the owner, Liz Glass.

"I know you're on a date," she said by way of greeting, "but I needed to ask you if you'd be available

Saturday. I need a photographer for the Sullivans' family reunion."

Erin politely stepped away to admire the post-sized photographs lining the walls of the lobby.

"I thought you already had a photographer booked for that one," Gideon said.

"I did. He backed out."

"Yeah, sure. Liam will be at his mom's this weekend, so I'm free."

Liz flashed him a grateful smile. "Thank you. I owe you for this. Give me a call tomorrow, and we'll work out the details. Ah, here's your picnic dinner. You two have fun."

"We will. Thanks." Gideon accepted the Styrofoam boxes from the waitress and stepped over to Erin, who was currently distracted by a photo of a stormy Tidewater Point awash in a moody gray that set off the faint peek of a ruddy sunset. "Ready?"

"Ethan said you took all these," she remarked.

"I did. Back in college on a trip out here with Dad. He sold them to Liz." He glanced from one photo to the next. "They were my first sale and the first inkling I had that I could make a career with my photography even though everyone thought I was nuts."

"They're stunning. You have an incredible gift."

"Thank you. Shall we?"

As he drove to the northern beach access, they talked about his photography and how he'd gone from an intern for a renowned photographer in San Francisco to a partner of another in Portland to owning his own business. While it was a topic he usually enjoyed, he didn't want to think about work this evening. He didn't want to think about anything but Erin and showing her that she wouldn't ever have to settle for half a relationship or none at all.

Gideon parked his SUV, but this time, Erin didn't wait for him to play the gentleman, so he walked around to the rear of his car after handing their dinner to her. When he slung his guitar over his shoulder, piled two blankets and a pair of throw pillows on his arm, and hooked the handles of a canvas grocery stack with his free hand, she laughed.

"Wow. You came prepared."

"Didn't want to leave anything to chance," he grunted, awkwardly closing the door with his elbow.

"I see that."

They made their way through the sand dunes to the beach, and because her driftwood fort seemed as good a place as any, Gideon settled his goods inside. He spread one of the blankets over the log in front of the fort, spread the other on the sand in front of it, and propped the pillows against it. Erin sat primly on the log with the Styrofoam boxes in her lap, watching as he dug six vanilla pillar candles out of the canvas sack, set them around their picnic site, and lit them.

"It's a bit warm for a fire yet, so these will have to

do," he remarked.

"You really *are* a romantic."

"What can I say?" he quipped. "I learned from a master. And I finally found a woman who makes me *want* to be a romantic."

He turned to her, set their dinner boxes on the blanket, and offered his hands to help her to her feet, then eased her into his arms. Lowering his head, he touched his lips to hers, tugging on her bottom lip as he pulled away. She followed him, and he took that as permission to kiss her again. With his senses heightened by the memory of their conversation on Sunday, he skimmed his tongue over her lips, noticed the tiniest tensing of her body, and backed off.

No tongue at all, he noted, brushing his fingertips over her cheek in a silent apology.

"Sorry," she whispered.

"Don't apologize. Never again—not for that. All right?"

With her lips pinched between her teeth, she nodded.

"Good. Dinner time."

He settled their dinner boxes on the blanket and slipped a bottle of sparkling cider and two plastic champagne flutes from the canvas sack. "Owen said you don't drink, but I wanted something festive to toast with."

"Any more tricks up your sleeve?"

"Mmm. A few," he replied noncommittally. He poured them each a glass of cider.

"What are we toasting?"

He lifted his drink. "To us... and never settling for half relationships again."

She was exquisite with that shy smile gracing her features. Lifting her glass and clinking it against his, she murmured, "To us."

They drank to each other, and Gideon liked the way she held his gaze as she did so. Despite the traumas in her past, she was still a strong woman, and he wished there was some easy way to tell her that that more than compensated for her limitations. But the best things in life were rarely easy, and words would never be enough. He had to show her.

He handed her the Styrofoam box with her name on it. "Another trick. I asked your brother what you liked to eat at the Tidewater, even though I swore I wouldn't cheat and ask him to reveal your secrets. Cheeseburger, huh?"

The last he struggled to say with a straight face. The Tidewater Inn's kitchen served up gourmet steaks and seafood, and with her own remarkable talents in the kitchen, he'd thought Owen was joking when he'd revealed Erin's favorite menu item.

"What?" she asked. "They're *really* good."

"I'm about to see if I agree. I ordered one myself, but with bacon."

141

"You won't be disappointed."

She was right. The burger was fantastic—cooked and seasoned perfectly—and it was *not* the run-of-the-mill burger he'd been expecting.

They ate in silence, enjoying their meal too much to talk. Gideon finished before Erin, so he wiped his hands clean, downed the rest of his cider, and reached for his guitar. He absently strummed a slow song of his own composition, watching a pair of kayaks rounding North Point. They were too far away for him to see who was in them, but he suspected it was Hope and Owen with Liam and Daphne.

Erin finished her meal and scooted over, leaning against him with her head on his shoulder as he played. A serene contentment radiated from her, soaking into him with blissful warmth and tempting him to set his guitar aside and let his fingers play over her soft curves instead. But the kayaks were approaching quickly, and the closer they came, the more certain he was about their occupants.

"We're about to be interrupted," he said, resting his guitar on the blanket.

Kicking off their shoes, they wandered down the beach to the water's edge, reaching it just as the kayaks slid onto the sand.

"Having fun?" Gideon asked.

Liam nodded vigorously as he crawled out of the kayak he'd shared with Owen. "Owen let me paddle, and we went all the way to the other end of North Star Beach. Oh, and we saw three seals and a couple sea otters!" Suddenly, he noticed Erin standing a few feet behind his father. "Oh, Erin! Wow! You're so pretty!"

"Thank you," she replied, leaning down to kiss his cheek.

"Tell me you guys aren't done already," Gideon said to Owen.

"Sunset isn't that far away, and we still have to feed the kiddos."

"Need a hand hauling the kayaks up to your truck?"

"Nope. You two just enjoy your date."

Gideon beckoned his son over and gave him a hug. "You're being good for Hope and Owen, right?"

"Uh-huh!"

"Good. I'll see you in a couple hours."

After Liam had zipped up the beach after his cousins and Owen, Gideon turned to Erin. "Still feeling guilty about not bringing him on our date?"

"Not so much."

"Mmm. Good. Because it'd be rather awkward and difficult doing things like this—" He yanked her into his arms and lowered his head to nibble on her neck. "—with him around."

She let out a shriek of surprise that quickly tumbled into giggles. If he'd ever heard a sweeter sound, he couldn't recall it.

He glanced westward. A storm brewed somewhere far offshore, and as the sun sank closer and closer to the ocean, it painted the approaching clouds in gold. The way it colored the world around him was magic, creating an air of romance and anticipation. With one hand still resting against the small of Erin's back, he dug his phone out of his thigh pocket, selected a slow, romantic song, and turned the volume up. With the phone safely back in his pocket, he slipped his free hand around Erin's and led her in the best waltz he could manage having never danced one before. She fell easily into step with him, unconcerned about the foamy waves washing over their feet. The moment was absolute perfection, like all the vibrations in the universe had settled into one exquisite rhythm.

"This right here," he murmured, "is all I've ever wanted."

"Dancing on the beach?"

"No. Being utterly in tune with my partner." He took her face in his hands and touched his lips lightly to hers, brushing his thumbs over her cheeks. Then he pressed his forehead to hers and let out a breath. "Kissing, dancing, even sex—none of it is truly intimate without this."

When he lifted his head, she was watching him with eyes widened with innocent desire.

"Did you ever experience anything like this with Chaz?"

She didn't immediately respond, but then, slowly, she shook her head.

"I never had anything like this with Hannah, either. Not once in eight years."

"Play that song again."

He did as she requested and was surprised when she slipped her hand around the back of his head and pulled his mouth down to hers. She kissed him more daringly than he would've thought possible after their heart-wrenching conversation on Sunday, and need thundered through him as she slipped her tongue between his lips. God, she was incredible. He angled his hips against hers, asking for more and hoping she could give it.

She tensed up like she had in Mendocino, and he inhaled sharply, breaking the kiss. She tried to kiss him again, but he leaned back, wincing as the confusion in her eyes quickly gave way to disappointment.

"I'm s—"

"Uh-uh. No more of that. Remember?"

She nodded, the shine of tears in her eyes broke his heart.

He slipped from her grip, sliding his hands town her arms until he reached her fingers, and brought her knuckles to his lips. "Slow and easy, *querida*. And if there are things you can't ever get past, we'll find ways to make up for it. Like this."

He resumed their dance, gratified when her tears

dried up and a joy as stunning as the deepening sunset above brightened her face. He opened his mouth to tell her that dancing with her was better than a kiss anyhow, but his phone rang. Growling at the interruption, he slid it from his pocket and glanced at the screen. His heart lurched.

Habit, he thought. "It's Hope."

"Answer it."

"Hey, cuz. What's up?"

"Liam is fine, but he fell asleep on the ride up to the house. Owen woke him up, and he's eating dinner, but he's not going to make it through a movie. Are you sure you don't want to let him spend the night?"

"I'm sure. We have to get up early to head into Beaverton tomorrow. I need to pick up Andra's birthday presents—the printer said they're finally ready. I'll come get him." After ending the call and dropping his phone back into his pocket, he sighed. "Looks like I need to call it an early night."

"Who says we have to end our date here?"

He lifted a brow. "Well, I need to go get him. Which means I'll need to take you home because once he's in bed…."

He let the sentence hang because Erin had flipped a switch and was now grinning shyly at him. "Why are you looking at me like that?"

"Maybe I could spend the night with you."

He regarded her with narrowed eyes. "Not yet.

You're not ready for that."

"What if we take sex off the table?"

"Tempting. *So* tempting." But he shook his head. "I only know one of your triggers, and I'm sure there are more, and I—"

She cut him off with a kiss, and he groaned low in his throat.

"You're *not* making this easy," he muttered against her lips. "I appreciate that you *want* to move things along. I do. But I don't want to screw this up. Okay? There's too much potential here to risk by rushing things."

He opened his mouth to add something else, but he couldn't find the words to adequately express the feelings her revelations had awakened. So instead, he folded her into his arms and sighed. If she hadn't experienced the traumas she had, he would've jumped at her offer, and once upon a time when he was young and stupid, he might've plunged headfirst into sex, but Erin was different than any woman he'd ever dated. She was strong but also fragile, and he cared too much for her already to risk joining the list of men who had hurt her.

"I wish we didn't have to cut this short," he whispered. "I could stand right here, with you in my arms, until the stars came out. Maybe even until the sun came up again, although I'm not sure my legs would appreciate that much."

She laughed softly at his attempt at humor. "We'd

better get our picnic packed up so you can get Liam."

"I'm sorry, Erin." He let out a huff of disappointed laughter. "Welcome to dating a single father."

"You won't hear me complain. I adore your son, Gideon, and believe it or not, the whole paternal thing is a major turn on. I don't have to wonder if you'll be a good dad because I already know you're a great one. Chicks dig that."

If she hadn't ended the statement with that quip, he might've cried in gratitude for this incredible woman. How could he be so certain she was everything he needed and wanted for the rest of his life when he'd known her such a short time?

He dipped his head to kiss her, catching her lower lip between his teeth and giving it a tug because she seemed to enjoy that, and was rewarded when she wove her arms around his neck and pressed the length of her body to his. It was amazing, really, that she was willing to push her boundaries after everything she'd been through.

She was just amazing, period.

As he released her and started gathering the remnants of their picnic, he snorted. Yeah, he was a goner.

Eleven

"WE'RE NOT GOING to let this ruin Andra's birthday party," Gideon said to his son as they trotted down the stairs and onto the path to Owen's house. "Not for us and definitely not for Andra. Right?"

Liam nodded sullenly in agreement but tears still gleamed along his lower eyelids.

"I'm sorry, bud. I truly am. I keep hoping...." Gideon shook his head. Talking about Hannah and his perpetually unfulfilled hopes for her relationship with their son was *not* going to make it easier for Liam to push her call from his mind. "Cake and ice cream and maybe a walk on the beach later. That'll be fun, yeah?"

Again, his son nodded. Gideon combed his fingers through the boy's silky dark hair, then pulled him against his side in a hug.

At least it wasn't hot today. In fact, it was almost cool enough to be called chilly. The blazing August sun was hiding behind a ceiling of dark clouds and a brisk, damp wind blew off the ocean. The waves were higher today, too, driven toward the coast by the storm system that had been lingering stubbornly off shore the last few days. Gideon wished the tempest would hurry up and get here. He could use the distraction of photographing the stormy ocean.

Liam was unusually silent for the duration of their walk, and Gideon's heart ached for him even as anger simmered. Even the prospect of spending the day with Daphne and Hope and Owen wasn't enough to cheer the boy up.

Owen stood in his open front door when Gideon and Liam arrived.

"Saw you coming," he said. "I'll take that."

Gideon handed him the gift for Andra and stepped past him into the blissful warmth of the man's home. A cheerful fire popped and crackled in the fireplace, and it did a lot to chase away the gloom. Andra and Red were already here. Since Red's sons Ethan and Ian weren't coming—they were holding down the fort at the Grand Dunes today, and it was booked—that made Gideon and Liam the last to arrive to the small, intimate gathering. They would've been twenty minutes earlier if Hannah hadn't called.

"I'm so glad you came!" Andra said.

She and Red left their seats on Owen's couch to embrace Gideon and his son, and their warm welcome did even more than the fire to soothe him.

"Sorry we're a little late. I had an unexpected phone call to deal with."

"Everything all right?" Red asked.

"Fine. Thank you. Are you *sure* you don't mind us crashing your family event, Andra?"

"You aren't crashing it," she assured him. She laid a cool hand against his cheek and searched his eyes with a faint smile playing about her eyes. "You're adding to it."

"Are those my boys I hear?" Erin called from the kitchen.

"Yep," he called back, unable to stop the smile from claiming his face. *My boys.*

Erin poked her head around the corner and grinned. It faded quickly when she met Liam's gaze. "What's wrong, sweetie?"

"You lied!" the boy replied, half yelling and half whining. "You said she loved me, but she doesn't! You lied to me!"

"Liam!" Gideon snapped and reached for his son's shoulder to bring him closer in for a more thorough reprimand. "You don't speak to Erin like that!"

Liam tore loose from his grip and raced to Erin. Frowning, she dropped to her knees and held her arms open. Gideon's mouth fell open when his son didn't hesitate to throw himself into them. He couldn't make out everything the boy said, but it sounded like he was repeating what he'd already accused Erin of, and each time he reiterated it, there was less anger in his voice and more tears.

"Hey," Erin murmured. She lifted her gaze to meet Gideon's. "It's okay."

He wasn't sure if she was talking to him or to Liam. Maybe both. Either way, it didn't matter. What mattered was the way his little boy had run to her, trusting that he could vent his frustration to her and still find comfort in her arms. Gideon stood, rooted to the spot and enthralled as she soothed his heartbroken son. After a few minutes, Liam straightened and nodded when Erin asked if he was better.

"What happened?" she asked, picking Liam up as she stood.

"What do you think happened?" Gideon replied.

"Hannah called... and she's not taking Liam this weekend."

"Bingo."

"Why?"

"Supposedly, a pipe broke and flooded her apartment," Gideon replied. "Fine. I get that. But that doesn't explain why she wouldn't take me up on the offer to stay at my house with Liam. I have a shoot at the Tidewater this weekend, so I wouldn't even be there."

"She doesn't want to see me," Liam mumbled against Erin's neck.

Her brows dipped briefly, but whatever thought crossed her mind, she kept it to herself. She leaned back to smile at the boy clinging to her. "Daphne's out on the deck watching the waves if you want to play with her. I promise we'll call you in when it's time for dinner."

Liam clung to her for another few seconds, and Gideon wondered if he planned to stay right there in her arms, but his excitement to play with his cousin won out, and he dropped to the floor and raced out the back door. A cool waft of air curled into the warm house in his wake.

"What can I do to help?" Gideon asked, wandering into the kitchen on Erin's heels.

"Well, if you're as terrible a cook as Hope insinuated after yesterday's cake-baking," she quipped, "nothing."

He pressed his lips into a self-mocking smile. "Drop one egg on the floor and suddenly I'm so bad I can burn water. Sheesh."

She laughed softly, and he felt himself lean into her vibrant aura. Though there was shyness in her eyes, she took his hands and tugged him into her arms without a trace of hesitation.

"Are you all right?" she murmured.

"Sure. I just got out of having to drive home to

Beaverton to give up my son for the weekend. I'm fantastic."

"You don't sound like it."

He sighed. "I just want her to step up and be there for him."

"I'm sure you do, but you can't force her to do it no more than Chaz could force me to enjoy sex."

"You think I'm being too hard on her?"

"Maybe so. But let's not talk about her anymore, okay? It's my mom's birthday, and I'm in a really good mood."

"Yes, ma'am."

When she turned back to the stove to stir the spaghetti sauce—homemade from scratch with all the ingredients picked from her greenhouse and garden, if he had to guess—he slipped his arms around her waist and rested his chin on her shoulder. To his surprise, she leaned back into him and kissed him over her shoulder.

"Uh-oh," Hope said, stepping into the kitchen. "That's how it starts."

"How what starts?" Gideon asked.

"Love. I seem to recall a night not unlike this one, standing at that very stove cooking with Owen, and he did that, too…." She craned her neck to peer into the living room and beamed—one of those sly, I-know-a-secret smiles Gideon had seen only rarely on her face. "Things spiraled out of control after that."

"If what you've found with Owen is out of control, I definitely need to let loose more often," Gideon remarked. Playfully, he nibbled on Erin's neck, and she let out a squeal that tumbled quickly into giggles. He grinned. "I'm glad that kind of touch is within your sphere of comfort because I can't resist it."

"You brat!" she giggled. "You made me slop sauce all over the stove. Hope, would you hand me the rag? And I think this is ready for tasting, if anyone wants to try it."

Hope didn't hand her the rag; instead, she wiped up the spill herself and then grabbed a spoon out of the drawer and dipped it into the spaghetti sauce. After letting it cool for a moment, she tasted it and purred. "Owen wasn't kidding. This is incredible, Erin. Can I trouble you for the recipe?"

"Sure. Remind me later, and I'll write it down for you."

Gideon snatched a spoon for himself, watching the two women as he waited for his taste to cool. There was no reservation in either of their demeanors, and if he were walking into this scene as a stranger, he would've guessed they'd been friends for years and not only a couple months.

"This is nice," he murmured. Then he slurped the sauce from his spoon and echoed Hope's earlier purr. "And *this* is amazing."

With dramatic flair, he dropped to one knee and held Erin's hand up. "Marry me, woman."

"What on earth is going on in here?" Owen asked, joining them in the kitchen.

Andra and Red walked in behind him, and both surveyed the scene with matching expressions of amusement.

"Gideon just proposed to your sister over spaghetti sauce," Hope replied, slipping her arm around Owen's waist and rising up on her toes to kiss his cheek.

"He *what?*" Owen asked, laughing. "You gotta make her work harder than spaghetti sauce. At least get her to make you her from-scratch double-decker pizza."

"Double... decker... pizza...." Gideon wiped the imaginary drool from his chin.

"You'll think you've died and gone to heaven," Red remarked.

"Is *that* all it takes to get a proposal out of you?" Erin laughed, sitting on Gideon's knee and draping her arms around his neck. "Interesting. It seems—despite what popular culture would have us women believe about sex being the way to a man's heart—the quickest way is still through his stomach."

"The old adage is wrong, too," he said, keeping his voice so low only she'd be able to hear. "The quickest—and also the securest—way to a man's heart is through his heart. Find out what makes his heart beat, and you'll have it for the rest of your life."

Her smile softened. "Hmm. Another interesting idea."

"Is it now?"

"Mmm-hmm."

He narrowed his eyes as he studied the smug but tender quirk of her lips—how was it possible to be both? "Okay…. Are you going to tell me why?"

"It's interesting because I'm pretty sure I know what makes yours beat."

Abruptly, she bounced off his knee and resumed her position at the stove, stirring the sauce and resolutely refusing to look at him again. He didn't have to ask what she believed made his heart beat; when she shifted her gaze out the doors to the deck, that was all the explanation he needed.

What would happen if he proposed to her in earnest right here and now?

"How much time on the sauce, sis?" Owen asked.

"Another fifteen minutes or so."

"Mom, would you mind opening your presents now? It's looking like rain out there, and if we all want a walk on the beach, we might want to get the rest of the party out of the way in a hurry."

"Fine by me," Andra replied.

"Gideon, would you mind bringing the kids in?"

"On it," Gideon said, rising to his feet at last.

He leaned outside and hesitated a moment before he called Daphne and Liam in. The storm was closer, and the scent of rain was heavy on the wind—heavier now than the salt spray. The two young cousins leaned on the deck railing, watching the surf crashing and cheering with the particularly big breakers. If Erin hadn't already put him in a better mood, it would've been impossible to remain rooted in frustration in the glow of their innocent delight at the storm's power.

"Liam, Daph," he called. "Come on in. Andra's going to open presents while dinner's cooking."

He wasn't the only one whose mood had improved. Liam grabbed Daphne's hand with a broad smile and raced with her toward the house. Gideon chuckled as he stepped aside to let them in.

This was what life was supposed to be about—celebrating birthdays, enjoying fabulous home-cooked meals with family and good friends, letting the vibrant joy of children remind him that the simple things in life made it worth living, and acknowledging the incredible forces of nature.

Speaking of forces of nature....

He sidled up behind Erin, who was still in the kitchen, and slipped his arms around her again. Lowering his head, he kissed her neck, pleased when she turned her head toward him again with a wide smile.

"See? Intimacy isn't always about sex," he murmured. "Most of the time, it's just being together. Like this."

"And you still think you'll be okay if this is the best the physical side gets with me? If this is the most relaxed and... *into it...* as I can be?"

"Erin, this is more than I've had with a woman in eight years. It may be more than I've *ever* had."

She snorted.

"I'm serious. And what's sad is that I don't think I realized what I was missing until now."

She tensed in his arms, and he released her. When she turned to face him with a thoughtful frown pinching her brows, he took a step back to give her space.

"Too much?" he asked.

"No…. I've just never—"

"Hey, lovebirds!" Owen called from the living room. "Get in here already. You're holding up the party."

Gideon's head sagged, dropping hard enough to elicit a complaint from the muscles in his neck. It appeared he'd have to wait to hear what Erin *had never*. Sighing, he offered his hand, and she twined her fingers with his. He lifted her knuckles to his lips.

They settled on the couch together with Daphne and Liam sitting on the floor beneath them, and Gideon was surprised when Erin tucked her feet under her with her knees resting on his thigh and pulled his arm around her shoulders.

Hope helped Owen bring the gifts to Andra. The first she opened was the handmade card Liam and Daphne had made for her at their dinner with Hope and Owen, and her genuine appreciation of the kids' card warmed Gideon's heart. Next, she opened the gifts

from Red's sons—high-end fishing gear that made Andra cheer with a delight similar to Daphne's and Liam's
watching the waves—that tied in with the two-day fishing excursion Red had bought for them both.

"Mine ties in with yours, Owen," Gideon said.
"So they probably ought to be opened together."

Nodding, Owen handed both gifts to his mother.
She unwrapped Owens's first—the shot Gideon had
taken of her and Red in the kayaks, and she laughed as
she studied it. Then she opened Gideon's gift, and
pressed her fingertips to her lips.

"You've captured Red and me perfectly," she said.
"But this one…."

She stared at the shot Gideon had taken of her
son and daughter—the one he'd known was perfect
even without looking—for almost five minutes. Then,
without a word, she strode over and wrapped Gideon in
a powerful hug.

"Thank you," she whispered. "I have no words
for how beautiful and how great a gift this is."

"I think what Mom is trying to say is that no one
has ever captured us and our love for each other so perfectly," Owen said. "It's beautiful, Gideon. Thank you."

"You're welcome," he replied. "Truly."

He swiped at his tingling eyes before they gave
him away. For a long time, Andra, Owen, and Erin had
only had each other, and instead of letting the hardships
of life fracture their love like happened to so many fami-

lies, they had used those hardships to fortify that love. He thought he'd understood that, but he hadn't. Not until this moment. He could search the world over and never find a greater gift than that photo.

Sensing Erin's gaze on him, he turned his attention to her.

So much for thinking the tears in his own eyes had gone unnoticed.

"Don't worry," he said. He meant it teasingly, but his voice was thick with emotion, and it edged the joking tone out. "I have a print for you, too. I'm just waiting for Owen to finish the driftwood frame. He'll will get one, too, as soon as he decides how he wants to frame it."

She gave him a watery smile, opened her mouth to speak and snapped it shut without a word, then buried her face against his chest. He tightened his arms around her.

"All right," Owen said, clearing his throat. "Since everyone is either already crying or on the verge, I might as well push us over the edge."

Owen stepped over to the hearth and plucked a tiny box from behind the family photos that adorned the shelf and took a knee in front of Hope. A collective gasp filled the room, but Hope grinned. This was the secret behind her smile earlier.

Gideon kept the suspicion to himself, certain the couple intended their engagement to be the best gift of all for Andra's birthday. Daphne didn't know, however, and she let out a squeal that could wake the dead. Owen chuckled and waved her over. The little girl melted into her mother's side and regarded her future stepfather with wide, hopeful eyes.

"When Sam and Sean died," Owen began, "it nearly killed me."

Andra let out a small sound that wasn't one of joy, and Gideon glanced sharply at her. Had Owen…? The matching expression on Erin's face—a brief flicker of pain—said yes, he had been tempted to take his life and might have even tried. The pain this family had survived….

"I thought I'd have to spend the rest of my life alone," Owen continued. "Until you both showed me that there was something on the horizon for me, something wonderful. A new family. Hope, will you marry me and be the bright future I thought I'd lost forever?"

"Yes," she breathed and held her hand out for the ring.

"And Daphne, may I have your blessing to marry your mother and to be your stepfather?"

The little girl launched herself into his arms. "Yes!" she cried.

The ring Owen slipped onto Hope's finger with Daphne's arms still locked around his neck was among the most exquisite and sentimental Gideon had ever seen—a round-cut diamond flanked by iridescent abalone shell.

While everyone hugged and congratulated Hope and Owen, Gideon slipped outside. Walking over to the railing, he gripped it and watched the waves and moody gray clouds. Everything was gray.

Everything but the brilliant light burning inside him.

It had been a long time since he'd been a part of something like that in there, and the last time, he'd been too young and full of adolescent brashness to appreciate it. After high school, he'd gotten caught up in the excitement and freedom of college life, and after that, he'd been so busy building his photography career into something stable and profitable that he'd missed a lot of birthdays and Thanksgivings and Christmases. And in the eight years he'd been with Hannah.... Well, he could admit now that he'd never been happy with her. His relationship had cast a shadow over the get-togethers with his family. Forget the ones with hers. Those had consisted mostly of sitting around watching TV, arguing about the latest celebrity gossip, or fighting about something that had happened years ago. Moments like those in Owen's house this evening were what had been missing from his life.

The door opened, and he wasn't surprised when Erin joined him at the railing and slipped her arm around his waist.

"Are you all right?" she asked.

"Yeah," he replied. "It's been too long since I've been part of something like that in there. I've missed it."

"So why'd you walk out?"

"I figured it would be smart to get some air before I said something I don't think either of us is ready for yet." He turned to her and clasped her face. With a gentle smile, he brushed his thumbs over her cheeks, then bent his head to kiss her. "Don't think too much on that right now, all right?"

She nodded. "No promises on that. But don't stay out here too long. Dinner's about ready."

"I'll be in shortly."

She laid a finger on his jaw, turned his face to hers, kissed him lightly on the lips. Then she was striding away. He watched her until she was once again ensconced in the kitchen and for almost two minutes after, mesmerized by the graceful, habitual motions of her body as she stirred the noodles, tucked the garlic bread into the oven, and tasted the sauce one last time. When his son ventured into the kitchen, it melted Gideon's heart when she pulled a folding step stool out from beside the refrigerator so Liam could stir the sauce.

The picture they made....

Gideon slipped his phone out of his pocket, and even though the shot wouldn't be nearly as good as one taken with his camera, he snapped the picture. Sometimes a snapshot was enough, and this was one of those times. The first of many more to come, he hoped.

Twelve

DESPITE HER BEST EFFORTS to heed Gideon's advice, she'd failed miserably to keep his words from her mind all through dinner. She'd had a little more luck during cake and ice cream—the kids' sugar-fueled enthusiasm was hard to resist—but now, following her family down the stairs to Hidden Beach, her mind replayed her conversation with Gideon again.

There was only one way to take his words. He was in this for keeps. Even after everything she'd told him.

"You're awfully quiet," he remarked as they reached the bottom of the stairs.

They hung back a few paces as their party headed toward the arch and beyond to the main beach. Liam and Daphne raced ahead, hooting and crowing and laughing as their voices echoed off the stone.

"Just thinking," she replied.

"That's obvious. About what?"

She hadn't sorted through her feelings about his earlier statement, so she said, "You and Hannah. I want to talk about this idea of you being too hard on her, if that's all right with you."

His brows furrowed and his lips flattened into a thin line. "Sure. Why not?"

She winced at the bitterness in his voice. "That's exactly what I was talking about. Your anger at her is taking over your life. We're all having a great time to-night, and now you're scowling at just the *mention* of her." His expression darkened further to perfectly match the brewing storm clouds above them. "If you want me to shut up about it, I will. I know I'm sticking my nose where it doesn't belong... except that, all else aside, I do care about you, and I've never been able to sit by and watch the people I care about suffer without trying to help even when there's nothing I can really do."

He didn't answer, and his body language—tight expression, hands stuffed in his pockets with his eyes trained on the damp sand—didn't give her much hope he was willing to let her say her piece. And that, she was certain now, was the problem.

"I get it. It's not my place." Then anger bubbled

up, and she added more sharply than she wanted to, "I'll shut up and we'll go on pretending this will just go away on its own and that it won't keep eating away at you until there's nothing left of that lighthearted sense of humor I so love about you."

Finally, he stopped and looked at her, still frowning. "So you *do* think I'm being too hard on her."

"Yes, I do."

"She hasn't exactly given me a wealth of reasons to be proud of her parenting skills."

"I know she hasn't. But—hear me out on this—I think I get her. She reminds me of how Chaz made me feel. Like, no matter how hard I tried to do and be what he wanted, it was never going to be good enough."

"That's nothing like this."

"Isn't it? She's afraid of failing and of disappointing you just like I was afraid of disappointing Chaz. When was the last time you said a kind word to her?"

"I can't remember the last time she gave me a reason to."

"Is that really true, or are you just in the habit of pointing out her failures?"

He folded his arms defensively across his chest, scowling.

Erin continued before he could formulate a response. "How do you feel right now? Attacked?"

"A little, yes." He shifted his weight, but his posture didn't relax. "More than a little."

"Imagine how you would feel if I kept talking to you like this. You'd start to feel pretty resentful, wouldn't you."

Grudgingly, he nodded.

"And then you'd begin wondering what the point of trying is when I don't even notice. By pointing out only your flaws, I am setting you up to fail. And that's what you're doing to her. She's given up trying to please you because she can't."

"It's not about pleasing me, Erin. It's about our son and making sure he's safe and loved and has what he needs."

"Agreed. But she was pretty young when she had Liam, right?"

He nodded. "Twenty."

"And you were twenty-seven or eight with your own business and a solid income by that point, yes?"

"I had to fight a lot harder for jobs then, but yes."

"Can you see where I'm going with this? Here you are, this successful, self-made man who obviously has his act together. You're older and more experienced in life, and she looks to you for guidance."

A tremor worked its way through his body like he'd encountered something unnerving, and his hands came up. "All right, I get it."

She remained where she stood while he wandered a few paces away. Then he stopped and stared up at the rock arch separating Hidden Beach from the main beach with his hands in his pockets. The rest of their party had long since disappeared through it, and as of yet, no one had thought to look back and see that she and Gideon weren't following. Figuring he needed some distance from her and the uncomfortable points she'd made, she resisted the urge to go to him and wrap her arms around him until his head and shoulders sagged in acceptance.

She was mildly surprised he let her hug him, but even though he did, there was a stiffness in his body, and she missed the easy way he always responded to her.

"You're angry with me."

"No," he sighed. "I'm not."

"Do you think I'm wrong?"

He didn't answer immediately, and as the seconds ticked by, each slower than the last, she thought he wouldn't. But then he shook his head.

"I honestly don't know. She's never shown me anything that says she genuinely *wants* to be a better parent. Or a parent at all. She's...." He sighed again and some of the tension left him. "I don't know. Not quite detached, but definitely clueless and pretty self-absorbed."

"That doesn't negate my point."

"No, I guess it doesn't."

He pulled out of her arms and wandered away again, closer to the arch. His dog came zooming through—soaking wet, of course—and after giving her a couple halfhearted pats, he sent her off to find the rest of their group. Turning back to Erin, he asked, "What are you suggesting I do?"

"Try focusing on what she does right instead of what she does wrong. Negative thoughts beget negative results, positive thoughts beget positive results, and all that."

"And what if you're wrong and she really is as apathetic as I think she is?"

"Then it'll still benefit you. You can't change the situation. You can only change your reaction to it."

"When did you turn into a walking motivational poster?"

She grinned as an inkling of his delightful sense of humor returned to his voice. This time when she slipped her arms around him, he folded his around her willingly and fluidly, and even the fine mist beginning to drift over the beach couldn't cool the warmth she found in his embrace.

"I know one thing for sure now," she murmured, resting her head on his shoulder. "I don't like it when you're mad at me."

He chuckled. "I wasn't mad at you."

"I know, but you weren't happy with me, either. Feels pretty much the same."

"Mmm. I can't promise I'll be able to be nicer to Hannah, but I'll try."

"That's all I ask."

"If nothing else, it'll be better for Liam if I'm not constantly fighting with her."

"Exactly."

He lowered his head to kiss her, then kissed her neck and took her hand, and they started walking again. Idly, Erin wondered how far behind they were now. They strolled in silence all the way beneath the arch and out to the main beach. Red, her mother, brother, Hope, Daphne, Liam, and Shadow were already halfway to where the Jewel River spilled shallowly across the sand before it reached the cove. Since they were already so far behind, Erin asked if Gideon wanted to just wait in the shelter of her driftwood fort for their families to return.

They stepped over the big log in front and sat together on the dry sand inside. The fort wasn't by any means waterproof, but it would shelter them from the mist that had coated their clothes and hair with tiny silver beads and it also provided a solid windbreak. Sitting half in Gideon's lap, Erin picked up a long stick and drew patterns in the sand.

"I love that you aren't afraid to speak your mind with me," Gideon said quietly.

"Believe me, this is a new development."

"Then I appreciate it even more."

"Even when it's something hard for you to hear?"

"Especially then. It makes me feel like I'm not in

this alone." He tilted her face toward him and skimmed his fingers along her jaw with such tenderness that she shivered. "I know you're there to catch me when I slip."

She caught her lip between her teeth. His words on Owen's deck returned to her mind along with a potent desire to explore what they meant, but she still hadn't had enough time to work through the feelings they evoked, so she leaned toward him, slowly. Then she gave in to the urge and kissed him, tugging on his lip when she pulled away.

He dove after her mouth, and she tensed, fearing what was to come. But it didn't. He didn't try to coax her into opening to a deeper kiss and didn't try to force his tongue into her mouth like Chaz would've. Instead, he was content to work her lips—first the bottom, then the top—as he slid his hands over her shoulders and splayed them across her back to pull her body closer. Once she realized her boundary wouldn't be breeched, she relaxed and let the sensations of his caresses ripple through her.

Instinctively, she arched into him, and it stunned her. She'd never—*never*—done that before.

"Atta girl," he whispered, trailing kisses from her mouth to her jaw and down her neck to the curve of her shoulder. He shifted his hands and slid them under her windbreaker, skimming his fingers over her ribs higher and higher until his thumbs brushed the sides of her breasts. "Still safe?"

"Mmm-hmm."

"May I go a little further?"

"Mmm-hmm."

She wished she could tell him how powerful she felt at his words, like she was the one in control, and how respected he made her feel.

When he slipped his hands beneath her fitted tee, her body went rigid and the breath sucked through her teeth.

"Too far," he surmised.

"No. Your hands are cold."

He tugged her shirt's hem back into place and let out a sigh. Then he chuckled.

The spell was broken, but she tilted her head. "That was... good. That was progress. Think we could try again?"

"That's probably enough for now, I think. It might be best to end with you wanting more."

He leaned against the back wall of the fort and pulled her with him, tucking his arms snugly around her. With the tingles of his kiss and caresses lingering, she was glad to remain in his embrace to enjoy the firm warmth of his body. Content, she laid her head on his chest, mesmerized by the beat of his heart and how it slowed into a steady, relaxed rhythm as she listened.

"I definitely want more," she murmured.

"I appreciate that, but I don't want to push you and risk making a mistake that will ruin what was a wonderful moment."

His voice was a pleasant rumble beneath her ear, and she let her eyes drift closed as peace wafted through her. She could happily stay here like this with him for the rest of the evening. He trailed his fingers lightly over her shoulder and upper arm, lulling her into the twilight between consciousness and sleep. Tender affection for this patient man curled through her.

Was this what love felt like?

She thought she'd loved Chaz, but now she wasn't so sure, because even at its best, her relationship with him had never left her feeling simultaneously so fulfilled and so hungry for more. She didn't want this moment to end.

And as soon as she admitted that to herself, she realized something else.

All those clues this evening—the joking proposal in the kitchen, the comments about the key to a man's heart, and the remark out on the back deck—that had led her to the conclusion that he was in this for the long haul now brought her another realization.

She wanted it to be true.

She didn't get the chance to ask; the jingling of dog tags alerted them to Shadow's imminent arrival only seconds before she bounded gleefully into the fort and promptly showered them with sea water and sand as she shook. Erin's surprised shriek and Gideon's yells of outrange quickly descended into laughter.

"Good girl, Shadow," Owen said, peering into the fort. "You found them."

"Oh, yeah, she definitely found us," Gideon remarked. He tugged the neck of his T-shirt up to wipe his face.

"You two planning to stay in here all night? Because the rain's starting to come down now."

"Tempting." Erin glanced past him. And it was. But the storm had arrived at last. Sighing, she rolled to her feet. "A dry couch in front of a warm fire sounds pretty good, too, though. You coming, Gideon?"

"Yep. Get off me, dog," he grunted as he shoved against his black Lab's chest. He stood and stepped out of the fort, brushing the sand from his backside. Turning to Owen, he said, "I have a favor to ask of you and Hope, anyhow, that I forgot about in all the festivities."

"Anything you need, just ask."

"Well, I have that family reunion to shoot at the Tidewater Inn on Saturday, and since Liam isn't going to be with his mother in Beaverton… I need someone to watch him."

"I have a better idea," Erin interrupted. "Why don't *I* take him? He still hasn't seen my greenhouse yet. And it'd be a good bonding opportunity for us."

As soon as the words were out of her mouth, she snapped it closed. It wasn't her offer to take Liam for the day that surprised her—she would've done that, anyhow, even if Gideon was only her friend—it was how she'd phrased it.

"I thought you had to work this Saturday," he said.

"Nope, *next* Saturday."

"That'd be great, then. Liam will love it."

Owen glanced between them with a broad grin. When she gave him a pointed look to tell him to keep it to himself, he chuckled and turned to offer his arm to his fiancée as she and the rest of the group reached them.

"Hey, Liam," Erin said. "What do you think about spending Saturday with me in my greenhouse?"

"Really?" He gripped her hand. "You mean it?"

"I do. Your dad has that shoot at the Tidewater, so I figured you and I could hang out. And Daph can come, too, if you'd like and if it's okay with Hope."

"Fine by me," Hope replied. She beamed up at Owen. "That'd give us some alone time."

"Looks like you'll owe me for once," Erin told her brother with a wink.

"If this—" He gestured between her and Gideon. "—goes where I think it might, I think we'll be even. At last."

Erin slipped her arm around Gideon's waist and leaned her head on his shoulder. "Guess I'd better not screw it up, then, huh? Because I'm tired of owing you."

Thirteen

WHEN THE BOISTEROUS Sullivan family broke for an afternoon snack, Gideon found a quiet corner to catch his breath. Family reunions weren't his favorite jobs—the organized chaos, all the ducking in and out of people constantly on the move, and trying to avoid getting hit with the various projectiles from the games was exhausting—but after a couple weeks of not working, it felt good to be back in the proverbial saddle. It was still cool after the rain Thursday evening and yesterday morning, and enough clouds lingered to diffuse the sharp August sunlight. All in all, it was a great day for a shoot.

He nodded his thanks when Liz brought him a hearty roast beef sandwich and a large glass of iced tea.

"Thanks again for taking this job on such short notice," the owner of the Tidewater Inn said.

"My pleasure."

"Is there anything else I can bring you?"

"This is great. Thanks."

Not two seconds after she'd left him to eat in peace, his phone dinged with a new text message. He slipped it out of the thigh pocket in his khaki cargo pants and smiled.

Making pizza for dinner, Erin had sent. *Need to know when you'll be home.*

Rather than text back, he called her. She answered almost immediately, and he guessed the phone must've still been in her hand.

"The double-decker pizza Red told me about at Andra's birthday?" he asked by way of greeting.

"Sure," she replied. "Sorry. I didn't mean to interrupt your shoot. That's why I texted."

"I'm on a break at the moment. Everyone's refilling the tanks for the last hurrah of the afternoon. It'll probably be another three hours before I'm done here."

"Perfect. That gives us another hour or so before we need to start the dough to have it ready so you can help us top it when you get home."

When you get home.... As if her house and not his place in Beaverton or even his family's cottage was his home. He wondered if she would realize what she'd said. Probably not. "You even make the dough from scratch?"

"You bet. Why do you think Red loves it so much?"

"How's everything going? Is Liam behaving himself?"

"He and Daphne have both been fantastic. We're having a blast. Here. Liam! Your dad's on the phone."

A moment later, his son's voice came on the line. "Hi, Dad! How's the shoot?"

"Good. Sounds like you're having a great time with Erin and Daph."

"Yeah! We spent all morning in the greenhouse and she taught us all about how she set it up to grow all year. And I got to eat a mango right off the tree!"

Gideon grinned, remembering the mango she'd treated him to the day after he'd arrived. "Delicious, aren't they?"

"Oh, man."

Liam described in detail everything they'd done this morning, and Gideon chuckled at his son's enthusiasm. What he wouldn't give for this to be their life, to call home on a break during a shoot to hear all the fun things Liam and Erin had done together. Or to attempt putting together some kind of passable dinner for Erin to come home to when she got off work at the Salty Dog. He chuckled at that. He definitely needed to take her up on the offer to teach him a few of her recipes.

"I'm glad you guys are having fun," Gideon said.

"I can't wait to get home and join you. Hey, can you put Erin back on the phone? I'm going to have to get back to work in a minute."

"Sure. Erin, Dad wants to talk to you."

Shuffling filled the other end of the line and then she was back. "Gotta get back to work?"

"Yeah, pretty quick. Thanks again for taking Liam today. Not just because it helps me out but also because he needs this, to feel like he matters." In danger of being overwhelmed by emotion, he cleared his throat. "Is Daph staying for dinner, too?"

"Actually, she'll be staying overnight. I have an idea, but I'll talk to you about it when you get home."

There it was again. Home. Almost like she was trying it on for size.

"I can't wait."

He ended the call with a curious anticipation pulsing through him. With no way to guess what her idea might be, he shrugged, scarfed his sandwich, drained his iced tea, and carried his dishes over to the tub Liz had placed on one of the banquet tables for the Sullivan family. Several members of the family had finished their snack and were currently ooing and awing over the newest addition, a three-week-old baby boy. As Gideon framed the shot, he tried to remember when Liam had been that small. It seemed like another lifetime. So much had changed in the last year that those memories had begun to feel disconnected, but after his talk with his son and Erin just now, they were sharper, if only for a few moments.

How different would those experiences be with Erin? Would they be thrilled to learn of her pregnancy rather than filled with dread and resignation? And how wonderful would it be to look forward to the birth and to mark each milestone together?

His phone rang, and he stepped away from the Sullivans. Thinking it was Erin again, maybe assuming he was still on his break, he answered it without glancing at the screen—his eyes were still trained on the newborn.

"Don't tell me you've changed your mind about letting me help top the pizza," he teased. "I promise, I can handle it."

"Uh, what pizza?"

As if someone had dumped a bucket of ice water over him, his mood crashed. "Hannah."

"Yeah. Who'd you think it was?"

"Erin."

"You're still seeing her."

It wasn't a question, and the dismissive way she said it made his lip curl. "Yes. I am. And it's great. Thanks for asking."

"You don't have to be a dick about it. I'm just calling to see if you have any plans for Liam's birthday, because I'd like to do something fun with him if you don't. I need to know soon so I can request the time off from work."

Out of habit, he started to ask why she had to wait until his birthday to want to do something fun and why she couldn't have done it this weekend like they'd planned, but Erin's words to him during their walk on the beach Thursday rushed through his mind. Asking about Liam's birthday without being prompted and without waiting until the very last minute was a good thing. And also asking about *his* plans rather than simply making her own and expecting him to fall in line with them was good, too. It was progress.

He inhaled, held it to a count of five, and let it out slowly. "My dad was talking about coming down, but nothing's set in stone. If you take Liam *on* his birthday, we can celebrate with him that weekend. That might work better for Dad, anyhow."

Silence greeted him from the other end of the line, and for a moment, he wondered if the call had dropped.

"Are you still there?" he asked.

"Yeah. I'm just surprised you aren't yelling at me for backing out of this weekend. I really didn't want to, you know. But I had three inches of water all through my apartment, and I had to deal with that."

"I get it. And I'm sorry I was so hard on you about that." He started to add that he was so used to her backing out of plans and making up excuses that he'd overreacted, but his temper was rising again, so he swallowed the words. "I need to stop being so hard on you."

More silence.

"I can't promise I'll be able to change as quick as flipping a switch, but I'll try to be better. Good enough?"

"Uh... yeah. I guess. So, what about Liam's birthday?"

"I don't know yet. And I don't have time right now to discuss it. I'm in the middle of a photo shoot. I'll talk it over with Dad and Liam and Erin tonight when I get home, but I'd like for him to spend his birthday with you."

"Do you really mean that, or are you just saying it?"

"I really mean it," he replied before he had long enough to think about it and change his mind. "I have to go. I'll call you tonight."

"All right. Bye."

The line went dead, and Gideon slid the phone back into his pocket. That had gone better than he'd expected, and he didn't feel nearly as drained and angry as he usually did after he talked to his ex. He was going to count that as a win.

The next three hours flew by, and even as infectious as the Sullivan family's celebratory mood was, Gideon was worn out by the end of the shoot. He'd dropped Liam off at Erin's just after seven this morning, and it was now almost seven. Almost twelve hours. With relief making his body feel a bit like jelly, he packed up his gear, made arrangements for payment and delivery of the digital files and prints, and drove away from the Tidewater Inn.

He parked his SUV in the carport beside Erin's car and tapped into his reserve of energy to bound up the stairs to her door. He knocked, but hearing music, he doubted she could hear him, so he cautiously opened the door. As soon as he did, he laughed at her choice of music—one of the Pirates of the Caribbean soundtracks. The third, he thought. The warm, yeasty aroma of rising dough and the heartier fragrance of the sauce filled Erin's home, and he inhaled deeply as he stepped around the wall that separated the wide living room from the dining room.

The sight that greeted him was so beautiful that he quietly backed out of the house and fetched his camera from his car. When he returned, Erin and the kids were still in the same place, rolling out the pizza dough with their backs to the front door. He adjusted the settings on his camera, framed the shot, and pressed the shutter button once, twice, three times. Then he called out to them and pressed it again when they all looked around.

"Pirates of the Caribbean?" he asked loudly enough to be heard over the stereo. "Really?"

If the picture they made with their backs to him

had been incredible, the beaming grins they turned on him were brilliant enough to melt the polar ice caps. And this time Erin's smile didn't cool as it had after he'd taken the picture of her and Owen on the log in front of her driftwood fort. This was what he'd wanted then—to be the focus of her adoration.

It was breathtaking. He wanted to wrap it around himself and hold onto it for the rest of his life.

"You're home," she greeted, wiping her hands on her apron as she closed the distance between them and wrapped her arms around his neck.

"I'm home," he murmured. When she leaned back in his arms, he kissed her lightly on the lips.

Then his son was at his side, and he picked the little boy up for a bear hug. "Hiya, bud."

"Hi, Dad. Can we watch Pirates of the Caribbean now? Erin said I had to wait to ask you."

"Sure. But how about we wait until the pizza's in the oven so we can all watch it together?"

"That's what I meant."

"Oh, okay," Gideon laughed.

"How was the shoot?" Erin asked.

"Fun. Long. Mostly fun. It felt good to be working again. Even better that I knew Liam was here having a good time with you and Daphne."

"We definitely had a good time, didn't we, kiddos?"

"Yep," Daphne and Liam responded together.

185

Then they told him how much fun it had been to make the pizza dough, especially the part when they got to punch it. They talked so fast that Gideon's tired mind couldn't keep up, and Erin finally shooed them back into the kitchen to finish grating the cheese.

"You look tired," Erin remarked sympathetically. "But happy."

"That's an accurate assessment. I've been on my feet all day, and it's been a while since I've had a shoot like that. But it was good."

"The Sullivans are a riot."

"They are indeed. I laughed a lot. And I think I got some great shots they'll love."

"If they're even half as good as the one you took of Mom and Red or the one of Owen and me, I know they will." She nodded her head toward her couch. "Thank you for the print, by the way. I hung it up today."

He followed her gaze, and sure enough, there it was. Tilting his head, he smiled. It was definitely one of his finest shots, if not *the* finest. "That's a good spot for it."

"Mmm. So, hey." Erin turned abruptly to him. "I didn't know Liam's birthday was next Wednesday. We need to do something for him."

Just a week and a half away? It was that close? Suddenly, he remembered Hannah's call and was amazed he'd forgotten it. That was a testament to how right Erin was that he needed to change how he interacted with his ex.

"Yeah. I didn't realize it was that soon. Dad and I have been talking for weeks about him coming out for a couple days."

"Oh."

The way her face fell in disappointment was adorable.

"That'll be great, because then he'll get to meet you and your family. Think everyone would be up for another beach party?"

"You know us," she replied shyly, taking his meaning. "We're always up for a beach party."

He leaned down to untie his lightweight work boots. After he'd kicked them off, he set them near the door beside his son's. If his feet could sigh in relief, they would've. "I have a dilemma, however. Hannah called right after you did to ask if she could take Liam on his birthday. I said I'd call my dad to see if the weekend would work better for him."

Her brows rose.

"Yes, I followed your advice. I was nice to her."

"Good for you." She grinned with only a hint of smug *I told you so*. "So… I guess you need to call your dad."

"And what if it's too late for him to change his plans?"

She tilted her head and pursed her lips. "Why are

187

you asking me?"

"I'm asking because just now when you welcomed me home, I felt it." He stepped close enough to pull her into his arms. He couldn't be sure if she was testing his dedication to their relationship or if she was asking if he *was* dedicated to it, so he took her face in his hands. "I'm asking because I have hope that this is the real deal."

Before she could think too much on that, he lowered his mouth to hers and kissed her firmly. It wasn't easy to restrain himself and be satisfied with a playful tug on her bottom lip, but he managed, and the way she reacted—angling her hips into his and curling her hand in his hair at the back of his head—was incredible.

"Now that we've cleared up why I'm asking you," he said huskily, "what's your answer?"

"Invite Hannah out here. She's obviously trying if she called you about Liam's birthday, and that's a good thing."

"Don't you think that'll be awkward?" As soon as the words were out of his mouth, he recalled how masterfully Erin had handled Hannah the first time they'd met, in Mendocino. "Never mind. As long as you're sure you're okay with it, I will find a way to make it work, too."

"Make your phone calls, Gideon. The kids and I will finish the pizza."

He reached down to his thigh pocket for his

phone, but it wasn't there.

Erin laughed. "You left it out in your car again, didn't you."

"It would appear so. I'll be right back."

She grinned as she kissed his cheek and returned to the kitchen to help the kids put the toppings on the pizza. He didn't bother putting his shoes back on and slipped outside in his socks. Sure enough, his phone was sitting in plain sight on the passenger seat. He couldn't even remember dropping it there. Rather than go back inside, he slid into his car and dialed his father's number.

"How was the shoot?" his dad said, skipping over the standard greeting.

"Long but great. And fun. Hey, I talked to Hannah today, and she'd like to take Liam for his birthday. Is it too late for you to change your plans? I thought she could have him on his birthday, and then we and the McKinneys could have a beach party for him that weekend."

"I've already taken that Monday through Thursday off, and we're shorthanded as it is right now. There's no way I can change it."

Gideon cursed under his breath. "I was afraid of that."

"I guess she'll have to adjust her plans for Liam's birthday, won't she, since she waited so long to make them."

Was that how he sounded when he talked to Hannah or about her—sharply derisive? His lip curled. No wonder Erin had suggested he try being nicer to her. "This is well in advance of what she usually does."

"I suppose you're right. You're not thinking about inviting her out there for his birthday?"

"I am."

"Something happen with you and Erin?"

"Only good things," Gideon replied with a grin. "She told me I needed to be nicer to Hannah, and she's right. And until she pointed it out, I didn't realize how bitter I've become throughout this custody fight, Dad. I don't want to be like that. I want to be happy and to enjoy what I have with Erin. So, as long as you're not opposed to Hannah being here…."

His father sighed. "I'm not going to say I'm looking forward to it, but if you and your lady can bear it, I will, too."

"Thanks, Dad."

"Erin's getting you to make some positive changes, it sounds like."

"Yeah. She is." His smile deepened. "I like that she isn't afraid to put me in my place. Makes me feel like she'll be the partner I always hoped Hannah would become."

"That's good, Gideon." His father laughed. "That's better than good. It's great. So, should I bring your mother's ring with me?"

"I think so." The words were out of his mouth before he had fully comprehended his father's inquiry.

Matthew had another call, and anxious to head back inside, he promised he would call later when he had solid plans for Liam's birthday. He sat in his car for almost two minutes after pondering how quickly and easily he'd answered his father's question. His response didn't surprise him. He hadn't said it yet, but he loved Erin, and he knew it with a certainty that his father—the grand champion of short courtships—would be proud of.

Glancing at the phone still in his hand, he dialed Hannah to extend the invitation. Luck was with him; she didn't answer. He left a message to the effect that she was welcome to spend a couple days in Sea Glass Cove with the whole family, and if she didn't like that, she could rearrange her plans and take Liam for the weekend or not at all. He was kind about it, but he was done scheduling his life around her.

He snuck into the house and slipped his arms around Erin's waist before she or either of the children realized he was back, and the squeal of surprise that descended quickly into giggles brought a smile of pure joy to his face.

"So," he murmured in her ear, "what was this idea you wanted to ask me about?"

"I thought it would be fun to have a campout in the living room with the kids." She twisted in his arms to face him. "That is, if you and Liam and Shadow want to stay."

"Oh, can we, Dad?" Liam asked. "Please?"

He chuckled. "That depends. Do we get to make a blanket fort to sleep in?"

"That's the plan. I figured we could build it while the pizza's in the oven."

"In that case—" He lowered his head to kiss her. "—I'd love to, and I'm sure Liam would, too. We can run back to the cottage to get Shadow and Oliver and an overnight bag after dinner."

"Thanks, Dad!"

"Yeah, thanks, Gideon," Daphne replied. "This is gonna be so much fun!"

"Don't thank me," Gideon said. "Thank Erin. It was her idea."

Liam and Daphne hugged her at once, and she laughed. "You're welcome."

Gideon stepped away to snatch a pepperoni and watch the trio with fascination. He couldn't think of a better way to spend his evening after a long shoot. As if it hadn't already been incredible to focus wholly on his photography and the job and know that Liam was in good hands.

This right here—this was what he wanted for the rest of his life.

Fourteen

ERIN SMILED, GAZING at the two children sound asleep beneath the canopy of their blanket fort. They'd drifted off into the land of dreams almost an hour ago, and she'd tucked the pure, soothing joy of watching them sleep around her as securely as Gideon had tucked the blankets around them. Shifting her gaze to Gideon, her smile deepened. He lay on his side with his head pillowed on his arm, curled around his son in such a way that he couldn't be comfortable, but his eyes were closed, and he looked the picture of contentment. He wasn't asleep, too... was he?

She nudged him, and he only grunted.

"Gideon," she whispered.

"Hmm?"

"They've been out for a while now."

"Mmm-hmm."

"You don't seriously plan to sleep out here on the floor with them, do you?"

"Wasn't that the plan?"

"It was... but not anymore. I have something else in mind for us."

His eyes popped open. He was fully alert now, frowning, and he twisted toward her, propping himself up on his elbow to wait for an explanation.

She couldn't give him one. Admitting what she wanted out loud would kill the shimmer of heat that had been building all evening, and she didn't want to kill it. She wanted to ignite it.

"Come on," she whispered.

"They'll be bummed if they wake up in the morning and we aren't in the fort with them."

"We can set an alarm and sneak back in. They'll never know."

She rolled out of the fort and stood, waiting for him to join her. After almost a minute of indecision, he crawled out after her and commanded his dog to stay. The black Lab eyed him with a look saying plainly that she had no intention of abandoning her snuggle fest with the kids.

That was nice, too, having a dog in the house, and suddenly, Erin wished she hadn't decided that she worked too much to have a pet.

Threading her fingers with Gideon's, she pulled him out of the living room and down the hall to her bedroom. She'd left the mini Christmas lights on her canopy plugged in earlier when they'd dragged blankets and pillows for the fort out of the closet, and their soft light illuminated the frothy fabric of her bed. She took a deep breath and let it out, then turned to Gideon. When she slipped her arms around his neck and pressed her body to his, his brows furrowed again.

"You're not going to let me talk you out of this, are you."

"You don't even know what *this* is yet."

He regarded her with a brow lifted. "You're blushing. And your eyes are…." He shook his head. "What you want is plain as day. Erin…."

"Don't tell me I'm not ready. I want this, Gideon. And I need it."

Nervousness shuddered through her as she waited for his response. He searched her eyes, probing deep into her soul, and she hoped he wouldn't notice how her hands trembled. If he doubted her resolve for even a second, he'd tell her no. She admired and treasured that, but right now, she didn't want his chivalry. Rebelliously, she wanted to set the whole world on fire with him, to burn away every last agonizing memory of Chaz and the realization of how much she'd come to hate him by the end even before he'd admitted to cheating on her.

Even if making love with Gideon tonight turned out to be an awkward mess, it would close the door on her relationship with Chaz.

Stubbornly, she held his gaze. Seconds ticked by, and he made no reply, but the muscles in his jaw flexed and indecision played out across his handsome face.

"What if *I'm* not ready for this?" he asked at last.

Her heart dropped like a rock into the ocean, sinking fast as doubt bubbled up. "Oh."

His lips quirked. "Once upon a time, I could've jumped into bed with a woman without a second thought, but those days are gone." With a disarming tenderness, he brushed her hair back from her face. "They ended when I met you, *mi vida.*"

That one she knew. *My life*, he'd called her.

He spoke again before she could begin to work out exactly what that meant.

"There's a reason we agreed to take it slow, to ease into the physical intimacy. I don't want to hurt you."

"You won't. I don't think you can."

"I still only know a couple of your triggers."

"That's why I need this—because there's only one way to find them. I wish I could just tell you, but I can't because I don't know."

"And you think it's a good idea to throw caution out the window and go crashing forward, to hell with the consequences?"

Traitorously, tears burned her eyes and slipped down her cheeks.

He gathered her into his arms, and she let out a breath. It felt so good right here, wrapped in his embrace with the warmth of his body and the steady beat of his heart easing the awkwardness. This kind of intimacy was so easy with him that she hoped the rest would be, too.

"I feel totally inadequate right now," he murmured. "I wish I could wave a magic wand and make it all go away for you. But I can't."

"It means everything that you want to." Steeling herself, she straightened and lifted her eyes to meet his. Those warm, dark eyes swallowed her, promising peace and comfort and respect. "But none of this changes my mind. I want to make love to you, Gideon."

Why did saying those words make her face warm? Why did her throat close up as if trying to prevent her from admitting that out loud?

"I can't even say that without squirming," she said with a sniff. Folding her arms tightly around herself, she walked to the bed and sat on the edge.

She was surprised when Gideon sat beside her. She sensed him watching her, but it took her a moment before she could bring herself to look at him. When she did, she inhaled sharply. Understanding was clear in his eyes. He knew why she needed him right now and why she couldn't put off taking their relationship to the next level.

"Sometimes it's better to face our fears head on," he whispered.

She nodded.

"What do you need me to do? How can I make it easier for you?"

"Turn my brain off?"

"Hmm. I think I can do that."

"How?"

"Lie on your belly, and I'll show you."

She did as he asked, slowly, wanting to ask what he was planning, but his smile said *trust me*, so she swallowed her uncertainty and acquiesced to his unspoken request. As his hands skimmed up and down her spine and over her shoulders, lightly at first but with gradually increasing pressure, she moaned. A massage. Genius. The tension eased out of her muscles beneath his strong and capable hands, and by the time he pushed her tank top up to run his fingers over her bare skin, she was utterly relaxed. She lifted her upper body, bracing herself on her forearms, and he obeyed, slipping her tank top over her breasts and shoulders and then over her head and down her arms. She did the rest, annoyed by the interruption.

She sighed when his hands resumed their pleasant kneading.

And then he lowered his mouth to her neck, and she shivered with pure pleasure as the whiskers of his goatee and his breath tickled.

"How's that?" he asked.

"Marvelous. Before I completely lose my head, there are condoms in the drawer of the night stand."

"When did you get those?"

"Yesterday."

He paused for a moment, and when she craned her head to the side, she noted the frown had returned to his face. Rolling onto her back, too aware of being bare breasted, she resisted the urge to cover herself up. A flash of indecision crossed his face, momentarily darkening his eyes, and for one achingly disappointing moment, she feared he would tell her they couldn't do this. That he didn't want to. Then he raked his gaze over her, and after the initial flare of shyness, his obvious appreciation of her body ignited a fire hotter than she'd ever felt.

"I don't believe I've seen you without a shirt," she said abruptly. "Even on the beach, you've always had a T-shirt on."

Taking the hint, he stripped out of the plain white T-shirt, and the breath sucked through her teeth. He was gorgeous with just the right amount of muscle definition—not chiseled but toned enough to tell anyone lucky enough to catch a glimpse that he enjoyed keeping his body in shape. She lifted her hand to touch him but hesitated.

"What's wrong?" he asked.

"I… I want to touch you."

"You sound surprised."

"I am." She started to say she'd never wanted to touch Chaz, that first her inexperience and shyness and then the revulsion had stopped her, but she refused to let her memories of her ex cast a shadow over this moment. "I'm okay with the more platonic touches—hugging, snuggling, even some kissing, but…."

Unable to put the feeling into words, she sat up and lightly slid her hand over his chest, fascinated. As her fingers slipped over his collarbone and up his neck, her lips curved. God, he had a beautiful neck. And it seemed somehow incongruous that his skin was so soft when the muscle beneath it was so firm.

She wanted his hands on her again as she explored the planes of his body, but she couldn't find the words to express that, either.

She didn't have to.

His hands slid up her ribs to caress her breasts, and she grinned triumphantly.

This was going to happen. He wasn't going to tell her no, that they shouldn't do this. He wasn't going to stop, and rather than the fear that usually accompanied the anticipation of sex, this time there was only elation and relief.

She knew what the difference was. He accepted that she had limitations and was willing to work with them. He respected her and respected that she wanted to make love to him and needed to. And that inspired trust. It made her want to not just break her inhibitions but shatter them.

Fifteen

GIDEON WRAPPED HIS FATHER in a bear hug, glad
beyond words to see him again. After a moment, Matthew held him at arm's length to inspect him. Satisfied,
he smiled.

"You look a lot better than the last time I saw
you," Matthew remarked. "Relaxed. Happy. I'm glad to
see it."

"You aren't looking so bad yourself, Pops."

"Well, happiness can be experienced vicariously,
especially through one's child." Matthew craned his
head to peer into the living room. "Where's Hannah?
That's her car in the driveway, isn't it?"

"Liam wanted to take her down to Hidden Beach.
You know, I'm glad we decided to surprise him. He was

thrilled to see her." Gideon stepped aside to let his father into the cottage. They strolled into the kitchen. Matthew's bags could wait a few minutes until they'd had time to catch up. "It was nice to see them together like that. That's all I've ever wanted from her."

"I'm glad, but don't let that dissuade you from seeking full custody. That boy needs to be with you."

"Don't worry. I won't. Can I get you something to drink? I have some Bud Light Lime in the fridge, some iced tea, water."

"I'd take a glass of iced tea."

Gideon pulled the pitcher out of the fridge and set it on the counter, then tossed some ice into two glasses and cut one of the lemons Erin had given him from her greenhouse and poked a couple slices into each before pouring the iced tea into them. He garnished both glasses with another slice of lemon and carried them both to the table.

Matthew accepted his and regarded it with brows raised and lips pursed. "Since when did you get so fancy with the iced tea?"

"It's a by-product of spending time with Erin. She makes everything a work of art."

"I can't wait to meet her."

"Not much longer. She said she'd be up at four to start dinner."

"We could've just called for delivery. She doesn't have to go through all this work to make pizza for your son tonight."

"Mmm. You won't be saying that after you've tried her pizza. Trust me. You won't ever want delivery again." Gideon took a long drink of his iced tea. "We won't have time tonight, but make sure you get over to see her greenhouse before you leave town. You'll love it."

"So you've said. Speaking of your lady—here." Matthew slipped a ring box from the pocket of his windbreaker and set it in front of Gideon before lowering himself into his chair. "Figured you might want to put that someplace safe before she gets here."

Gideon reached for the tiny box almost reverently. He opened it, and the breath sucked through his teeth as he sank into the chair across from his father. He hadn't seen his mother's engagement ring in years, but it was exactly as he remembered. It wasn't elaborate or expensive, just a round solitaire diamond set in a slender white gold band. What made it special were the prongs that held the diamond in place. They were shaped to resemble the petals of a flower—a nod to what had brought Matthew and Maria together.

The French doors onto the back deck opened, but Gideon's attention was solidly focused on the ring. He slipped it from its protective cushioning and turned it around and around, mesmerized by the flash and sparkle as it caught the sunlight streaming through the big south-facing windows of the dining room and by the thought of it gracing Erin's long, delicate finger.

"Might want to put that away, son," Matthew murmured.

"Put what away?"

He flinched at the sound of Hannah's voice. In a rush, he shoved the ring back into the box, snapped it closed, and tucked it in his pocket. His ex seeing it would *not* make for a good start to Liam's birthday celebrations, given the hints of jealousy in her voice whenever Erin came up in their conversations.

He was saved from having to respond when Liam burst into the cottage after his mother and threw his arms around Matthew's neck. "Grandpa!"

"Hiya, kiddo."

"Matthew," Hannah greeted curtly.

"Hannah," Matthew replied with equal coolness in his voice. He returned his attention to his grandson, and when he spoke, his love for the little boy radiated from him in sharp contrast. "My God, you've grown since the last time I saw you. You must be half a foot taller, I swear."

"Nah. Just an inch."

"How's my favorite grandkid been lately?"

"Good, but Grandpa, I'm your only grandkid."

"So you are. For now, anyhow."

"Yeah, for now." Liam leaned in close and whispered, "But I'm kinda hoping Dad and Erin will get married and have a baby. I'd love to have a little brother or sister."

"Mmm. That would be nice wouldn't it."

They'd spoken so quietly that Gideon almost missed the exchange, but Hannah was closer, and by the frown on her face, she'd heard every word clearly. Great.

Then he caressed the ring box resting in his pocket, and he was reminded of his promise to Erin. He would be nice to Hannah while she was in town. He wouldn't set her up to fail by assuming she would react poorly to him proposing to Erin. She likely would, but that wasn't the point. The point was that he owed it to himself, to his son, and to Erin to be cordial regardless of his ex's reaction. Because, in the end, what she thought mattered little.

If he could keep that in mind and hold to his promise for the duration of her stay in town, he might actually be able to make it a habit.

Reluctantly, he rose from his chair. He slipped into the den and hid the ring in the drawer of the desk. When he returned to the dining room, Hannah had poured herself a glass of iced tea. Liam sat in the chair beside his grandfather, and Gideon glanced pointedly between him and his mother. Finally, he asked his son what he'd like to drink, eying Hannah as he brought him a glass of chocolate milk. At least she had the decency to look sheepish and apologize.

"Anyhow," Hannah remarked. "Liam says we're

making pizza from scratch for dinner. Do you think Erin would mind if I helped? I'd love to learn how she does it."

Gideon was certain his expression matched his father's undisguised shock, and when Hannah glanced between them, she confirmed it.

"What?" she asked.

"Homemade pizza is a bit more work than you like to do," Matthew replied.

"I'm trying to turn over a new leaf, too—just like Gideon—and since Liam's brought up Erin's pizza at least half a dozen times since last weekend, I figured that would be a good thing for me to learn so he and I can make it together."

"Now I'm doubly shocked."

"You know what, Matthew? You can go straight to—"

"That's enough," Gideon snapped. He sought his father's gaze and held it. "From both of you. If I can find it in me to be nice, you can, too, Dad."

He glanced at his son, who had clamped his hands over his ears, and his heart ached. *This* was why he needed to stop being so hard on Hannah and fighting with her. Look what it was doing to Liam.

"You're right," Matthew said. "I'm sorry, Hannah. You wanting to make pizza with your son is a good thing, and I applaud you for it."

"Thank you."

Her voice was still too sharp for Gideon's liking, but he wasn't about to call her out on it. Instead, he drained the rest of his iced tea and set the glass in the sink. "Are we going to light the candles tonight? Liam and I never did."

"Can we, Grandpa?" the little boy asked, his worries suddenly forgotten.

"Of course. Do we have enough in the cottage or should I run down to the store and pick some more up?"

"We might need a few more. Hope replaced the ones she burned earlier this summer, but I've used a few."

"Why don't I do that while we're waiting for Erin to get here?"

Gideon almost begged his father to stay until Erin arrived so he'd have a buffer between him and Hannah, but on second thought, Matthew was more likely to start trouble than stop it. He dipped his head in acknowledgement, took his father's glass, and went to the sink to wash it and his own.

"How was your walk on the beach?" he asked after his father had left.

"Good," Liam replied. "Mom found some really pretty sea glass, and I found some shells."

"Mmm. Owen will be jealous about the sea glass. I'm glad you two had a good walk."

They lapsed into an awkward silence. Gideon

stood with his back to the sink and his hands braced on the counter, and Hannah sat primly at the table. Liam sat in the chair across from her, glancing nervously between his parents as if he expected them to erupt into argument again. It was a sharp contrast to the easy interactions with Erin, and Gideon hoped she'd get here soon and rescue him.

Hannah turned to Liam. "Why don't you bring in our shells and sea glass so your dad can see?"

As the little boy slipped outside to collect their treasures from the table on the deck, Hannah rose from her chair and joined Gideon in the kitchen, leaning against the counter across the space that was suddenly too narrow. He regarded her warily, habit making him wonder what trick she was about to pull.

"Don't look at me like that," she muttered. "I'm not going to jump your bones. I just want to thank you."

"Oh? And you couldn't do that with Liam in the room?"

"It's hard enough without an audience, all right?"

She fidgeted with her necklace, sliding the delicate silver cross to and fro on its slender chain. He'd bought her that necklace after Liam's birth… and she'd worn it once in all that time. Suspicion simmered. What was her reason for wearing it today?

"I know this is as awkward for you as it is for me, but it means a lot to me that you didn't let that stop you.

I'm glad we're all here for Liam's birthday. Even your dad."

"It's definitely awkward," he agreed. "But I'm glad you're here. Liam needs this. He needs to see us not fighting."

"For the first time since you kicked me out, I feel like we might actually be able to do this."

"Do what?"

"Come together for Liam when he needs us without fighting."

"You can thank Erin for that when she gets here. She's the one who pointed out that me being hard on you wasn't helping anyone."

Hannah sniffed. "Why am I not surprised? To hear Liam tell it, she's perfect. So why can't I hate her even though I want to?"

"Don't hate her. She's had her own hardships, just like you and me. More, probably."

"Ugh." She laughed softly. "Now I really want to hate her. But if she's really the reason you're being nice to me again, I won't ever be able to. Are you…. Do you want to marry her?"

He eyed her, wary again. "Why do you ask?"

"I saw the ring before you put it away—you weren't as sneaky as you thought. Is it your mom's?"

He nodded.

She turned her gaze out the window behind him, staring at the cove and coastline beyond with that distant expression of someone who wasn't seeing with her eyes, too consumed by her thoughts. "You haven't known her a month."

"My dad proposed to my mother after two weeks, and their love still burns even though she's been gone for almost thirty years."

Gideon flinched when Hannah reached for his hand, but grudgingly, he let her take it. When she gave it a squeeze and met his gaze with blatant in her eyes, his chest tightened.

"I hope she's smarter than I was."

Abruptly, she dropped his hand and strode outside. He stared after her with his mouth hanging open. Where had *that* come from? In eight years, he'd *never* seen that kind of compassion and regret in her eyes. Not once. If he had, things might've turned out much different.

Or maybe it wouldn't have mattered. Maybe it would've only dragged out the inevitable and made courteous interactions with her impossible. After months of fighting with her, he'd begun to fear that was how it would always be, that there was no hope of being able to talk to her without falling victim to his pent-up anger. But since he'd started dating Erin and she'd pointed out how focusing on Hannah's failures was having disastrous consequences, he had been able to take a step back.

A poisonous voice in the back of his mind wondered if this sudden gratitude and humility was just another trick, designed to lull him into a state of pity. They still had the custody meeting—on Monday, in fact, just six days away.

No.

He would *not* think like that. If it was a trick, he'd deal with it when it was revealed. In the meantime, he was going to follow Erin's advice and not immediately expect the worst from his ex. She'd shown him something he'd never seen from her before, something his heart said was real. And he was going to trust his heart. It had a far better track record than his head. It had told him photography was the career path for him, that Hannah wasn't ever going to be a grow-old-together prospect, and more recently, it had told him that Erin was everything he wanted.

He was still standing in the kitchen exactly as Hannah had left him when his father walked in the front door, laughing. It took a moment for his brain to come back online and figure out why Matthew might be chuckling—he wasn't alone. Then he heard Erin's voice.

"I swear, I'm not kidding. He really did drop to one knee in my brother's kitchen."

"That must be some incredible spaghetti sauce. All that time with Hannah and he never once even *joked* about proposing."

"It's a good recipe. I've been asked for it more times than I can recall. But the secret is the garden-fresh ingredients. It doesn't seem like a big deal to buy fresh from the store, but it makes a huge difference."

"I'll admit, I'm excited to see this greenhouse of yours. Gideon and Liam have both described it at length. Oh no, don't you worry about this. I've got it if you wouldn't mind closing the door. Smells delicious."

They rounded the wall that divided the kitchen from the living room with their arms laden with a number of bowls and pots and canvas grocery sacks.

"Well, I guess I don't need to make introductions," Gideon quipped.

At once when Erin met his gaze, his thoughts of Hannah and what tricks she might or might not be playing with him melted away. The innocent delight in his lover's sea-green eyes wrapped him in a blanket of soothing peace, and the vibrant grin on his father's face answered a question that had been burning in his mind for the last week and a half—would Matthew approve of her?

Obviously he did, and Gideon let out a breath in relief.

"Sorry, son," Matthew remarked. "She's quite a charming lady, your Erin."

My Erin.... He'd never get tired of hearing that or of the warm glow those words stirred. "She is indeed. What's all this?"

"I'll have to duck out early tonight. Mom's still fighting that cold, so I have to head in dark and early to do the ordering tomorrow." She settled her armload of bowls on the counter. "I did all the prep work at home today so we'd have more time to lavish the birthday boy with attention and games and whatever else he wants to do."

"Technically, tomorrow is his birthday *and* his party," Gideon remarked.

"So?"

He lifted his hands. "Yes, ma'am."

"Speaking of the birthday boy, where is he?"

"Out on the deck with Hannah. She, uh, asked to help make the pizza."

Erin regarded him with brows lifted. "I thought you said she doesn't like to cook."

"She doesn't. But she wanted to learn how to make your pizza with Liam because he loves it so much."

"Wow." She nudged him with her elbow. "See?"

"Yeah, yeah. You're right. Don't let it go to your head or anything. Um, you wouldn't mind giving her the recipe, would you?"

"Not at all. Now I'm sorry I made everything at home. Would you grab me a piece of paper and something to write with?"

"Sure."

Before he went to the den to grab a notepad, he ducked his head out the French doors. "Erin's here, so it's time to make the pizza."

As he walked across the house to the den, he heard his father say to Erin, "I'm going to set out the candles for tonight. Will you be all right by yourself with Hannah?"

"We'll be just fine, but thank you."

The thought that he'd found a genuine angel carried Gideon to the den and back. He set the notepad and pen on the counter and asked what he could do while Erin gave his ex an impromptu cooking lesson. She thrust a block of mozzarella at him, so he dug the grater out of the cupboard beside the oven and jerked his head toward the dining room table.

"Come on, bud. You can help me with this."

There had been a time—and not so long ago—when Liam would've moaned and whined about anything that resembled work, but he was all too happy to grate the cheese. Gideon sliced a few chunks off to make it easier for his son to handle, then sat back and watched. Had it been only a couple months ago that Liam had griped about helping clean up the dishes and kitchen the night Hope had made that incredible stew?

With his son occupied and nothing to do himself, his attention sidetracked to the conversation in the kitchen. His fears that tonight—the whole of Hannah's stay in Sea Glass Cove, really—would be awkward now seemed silly. He should've known. Erin had a natural graciousness that made her irresistible. Hadn't Hannah admitted that it was impossible to hate her even for someone with every reason to?

"No wonder Liam enjoys this," Hannah remarked. "It does sound like fun. And all the ingredients are local? Even the cheese and pepperoni?"

"Yep. All the vegetables come from my own garden, we have a local meat block that makes all their own sausage and custom meats on site, and a cheese artisan who makes the most incredible cheeses. For such a small town, Sea Glass Cove has some pretty talented residents."

"I didn't realize there was so much here."

"You wouldn't know it to drive through."

"I can see why Gideon wants to move here. And why he thinks it would be such a good place for Liam to grow up," Hannah remarked, lowering her voice so much that Gideon had to lean in to catch her words.

"It's a great place to grow up, that's for sure. It's a quiet community but active, the schools are great, and outdoor opportunities abound."

"You think like a mom. I guess that explains how you're so good with Liam."

"He's a sweet kid, and he makes it easy. You and Gideon have done a great job with him."

"I'm sure you don't think I had much to do with it…."

Gideon's head snapped around to the kitchen, ready to chastise Hannah.

"…But thank you."

"And *I'm* sure you don't know what I think so I'll tell you. I think you were in a difficult situation and you've done the best you could so maybe you should cut yourself some slack."

Hannah studied Erin with narrowed eyes, but then she lowered her gaze and murmured, "That means a lot, coming from you. I mean, you only know me through what Gideon's told you, and he isn't shy about pointing out my flaws. So for you to say that and say it like you believe it…. It means a lot."

"Gideon's hard on you because he just wants what's best for Liam."

"I know that. But it still hurts."

"I know it does. You ready to move on to the dough? It's not nearly as difficult as you might think."

"Yeah, I think I got everything for the sauce written down. Thank you for doing this."

"My pleasure."

Gideon's mouth fell open, and before either she or Erin caught him eavesdropping, he turned his gaze back to his son and sliced off another chunk of mozzarella for him to grate.

A waft of perfect late summer air swirled into the dining room as Matthew stepped inside. He bypassed the table and joined the women in the kitchen to listen in on Erin's final lesson about the pizza dough. Gideon tried not to gawk, but it was a struggle. He watched as they rolled out the dough, spread the sauce and cheese, and debated good-naturedly which toppings they should put on it without a hint of discord. Hannah and his father seemed to have reached an unspoken agreement to set aside their animosity for the evening, and Erin was her usual charming self. Liam was positively beaming.

Gideon waited for some spark to ignite the powder keg, but it didn't come. Not while they sat out on the deck waiting for the pizza to cook and not while they ate it and complimented Erin on her mad skills in the kitchen. It didn't come even when Hannah and Matthew volunteered to do the dishes together and ganged up on Erin to prevent her from doing them. Gideon thought he might fall out of his chair when Liam asked to help, too.

Then it was time to light the candles around the deck and in the windows of the cottage, and Gideon finally realized the explosion wasn't going to come. With the magic of his family's long-standing tradition aglow around him and dusk settling over the cove, he exhaled and let the peace of it all wash over him.

"It can't possibly be this easy," he remarked when Erin slipped her arm around his waist. His vision blurred, his eyes mesmerized by the dancing flames all around him.

"Why not?" she asked. "You know, when Hannah isn't being defensive, waiting to be attacked, she's actually quite nice."

"I swear, I've never seen this side of her." He

glanced down at her and smiled. "You seem to bring out the best in everyone around you. Especially me."

Her brows dipped momentarily, but before he could register what might have dimmed her enjoyment of the moment, she flashed him a brilliant smile. Then she tilted her head up, asking him to kiss her. He couldn't help but obey, and when their lips touched, the jolt of concern was forgotten.

Sixteen

GIDEON YANKED A T-SHIRT over his head as he shuffled into the kitchen with sleep still blurring his vision. The sun was up, but the light filling the cottage was golden. It was early yet. The rich aroma of fresh-brewed coffee tantalized him, and he almost expected to see the coffee making itself, but his father was in the kitchen. Gideon ran his hands back through his hair to comb it out of his face.

"You ever going to cut that mop now that you and Hannah are being civil?" Matthew asked, reaching into the cupboard for two cups.

"I'm getting used to it. And Erin likes it."

"Coffee?"

"Please."

"Mmm. Something tells me she couldn't care less how you wear it." Matthew poured the coffee while Gideon fetched the sugar and milk. "How long are you going to make me wait before you take the next step toward making her a part of our family?"

"However long she needs. She's had enough men in her life try to force her, and I refuse to be one of them."

His father sighed. "I guess I'll have to be patient and trust your judgment. But you *are* serious about asking her to marry you? I didn't bring your mother's ring here for a *maybe*, did I?"

Gideon accepted a cup from his father and added a little milk and sugar to it—it wasn't a morning to drink it harsh and black. "Erin isn't a *maybe*."

"Just checking. It's a gorgeous morning out. Shall we sit out on the deck and enjoy it?"

Gideon followed his father outside and inhaled deeply as soon as he stepped out the door. It was indeed a glorious morning... if he ignored the fact that his little boy was officially eight years old today. Liam was growing up too fast, and when he expressed that sentiment to his father, Matthew laughed.

"You're telling me? Seems like only yesterday I was lamenting *your* eighth birthday."

It was cool in the shadow of the cottage, so they set their coffee aside on the deck rail and moved the table into the sunlight. When Gideon took his seat with his cup hot in his hands and his bare feet propped on the railing, he smiled. The sea was a tranquil blue-green this morning with no wind-tossed white caps to mar that incredible color and only small waves breaking on the rocks and bluff.

This was the life.

But there was something missing. Two things, actually. Erin and Liam. If they were here, this moment would be simple, absolute perfection.

"When was the last time you and I had a quiet morning like this?" he asked.

"Can't remember. Years ago." Matthew sipped his coffee and gazed across the cove. "I don't think I've said it, but I think you're right to move here. It'll give you some space from Hannah."

Gideon nodded in agreement. "I think—I *hope*—things will be easier with her from here on out."

"I hope you're right. Having something good to focus on makes the bad so much less of a strain."

They slipped into comfortable silence, content to enjoy the morning, the coffee, and the simplicity of occupying the same space again. Their relationship had always been like that, though—steady and uncomplicated—and Gideon thanked his lucky stars that he'd been blessed with a father who gave him an example to live up to. Because he had, he'd been up to the task of raising his son. And he'd also recognized what a rare and incredible woman Erin was.

"Did I just hear a car pull up?" Matthew asked.

"Yeah, I think so."

He glanced at his watch. It was earlier than Erin had said she expected to be done with her ordering for the Salty Dog, but she might've finished early. It certainly wouldn't be Hannah with Liam. Grinning suddenly, Gideon set his coffee on the table, stood, and leaned over the railing, expecting to see Erin's car parked on the road in front of the cottage. But it was Hannah's.

"Color me surprised," he murmured. "Wonder what she wants."

"It's not Erin?" his father asked.

"No."

Moments later, Liam skipped around the corner of the cottage with his mother a few steps behind. Gideon's brows rose. Not only was Hannah up and about well earlier than he'd anticipated, she was also fully made up for the day. She *was* an exquisitely beautiful woman, and after last night, he could appreciate that again. She'd never again be as beautiful in his eyes as Erin, but it was a relief to see more about her than his frustration with her.

"You're here early," he remarked as she and Liam reached the deck. "I thought you two were going to laze around this morning."

"We were, but Liam wanted to see you."

The little boy raced up the steps, and Gideon stepped around the table to pick him up. He let out a long breath as the little boy hugged him tightly. It was heaven to have his son in his arms again even though it had been less than a dozen hours since he'd seen him last. A reminder that the custody hearing was only a few days away jolted him.

What if the court awarded Hannah custody? Could he live with that?

"And... I need to talk to you," Hannah added. She perched on the railing. "About Monday."

Matthew glanced between her and Gideon, then rose from his chair. "May I bring you a cup of coffee, Hannah?"

She regarded him with her head tilted and eyes wide. "Um, yeah. Thank you."

"Liam, why don't you come with me so your mom and dad can talk?"

"Okay. Is Erin here yet?"

Their voices were cut off when Matthew pulled the door closed behind them, and Gideon turned his attention on Hannah just in time to catch the flicker of hurt in her amber eyes.

"He adores her," she murmured. "And after last night, I totally understand why."

"She's an amazing woman." Shifting uncomfortably in his chair, he lifted his coffee to his lips and took a sip. "So, what about Monday?"

"I'm going to agree to your custody plan."

The cup nearly slipped from his fingers. "What?"

Her brows knitted together and she lowered her gaze to the table top. When she spoke, her voice was so quiet that he had to lean in to hear her. "You're right. I don't know how to be a parent. You do."

"Hannah…."

"I laid awake all night thinking about it." She lifted her head again with a defiant gleam burning away the shadow of agony in her eyes. "I love Liam, and I want what's best for him. And that's living here in Sea Glass Cove. With you. And with Erin. He'll have a real family."

He gaped and failed to form a response. She watched him for a long time with a vulnerability he'd never before seen in her expression.

"Say something," she entreated softly.

"Is this a trick?" he blurted.

"What?" She jerked back and her eyes rounded. Then she pinched her eyes closed for a moment. "No, it's not a trick. I mean it."

"I'm sorry, Hannah. I just…." He inhaled deeply and began again. "Habit."

"I probably deserve that."

"You kinda do. Where is this coming from? You've been fighting me for months, doing these crazy, selfish things like dragging Liam to your sister's house to spite me. Why the sudden change of heart? I'm sorry, but you see why I might think it's another trick."

She nodded. "I'm tired of fighting. I'm tired of

watching what it's doing to our son. I didn't realize what a snot he'd become until last night… when he wasn't. I didn't recognize that sweet little boy. This past couple of weeks, when you've been trying so hard to bite back what you really want to say…. It's shown me that we don't have to fight. We can find a way to make this work. I didn't think we could."

"Neither did I."

Matthew returned them with Hannah's coffee, and she accepted it gratefully. He didn't linger, slipping quietly back inside.

Gideon narrowed his eyes, still not sure he believed that the fight was really over. "So just like that, you're going to agree to my parenting plan?"

"It's a fair plan, and it'll be good for all of us to have a set routine. I need that as much as he does. I've had the best time with him yesterday, last night, and this morning. And I think it's because I know I'll have a break from trying and failing to be a perfect parent. As much as it hurts to admit it, I suck at parenting. Things that come so naturally to you just don't to me. But I'm trying, and stepping out of the way is the best thing I can do for him."

He couldn't breathe, and his heart ached. This couldn't be real. He raked his hands through his hair, curling his hands into such tight fists that his scalp complained.

"Gideon?"

"This…. This is what I've been waiting eight years for, to know you're willing to put Liam's needs first. Why…?" He couldn't say the rest out loud—*Why couldn't you have done this years ago?*—because Erin strode into view around the side of the cottage right then, and he was glad Hannah hadn't shown him what he'd needed from her. If she had, they might have found a way to stay together and he wouldn't have met Erin. And she was everything.

"Am I interrupting?" she asked, her smile fading as she glanced between them.

He didn't answer. Instead, he trotted to the steps, took her face in his hands and kissed her soundly.

"Well, good morning to you, too," she said. Laughter danced in her eyes.

"We're almost done here, I think. I'll be in in a minute."

As she turned to go in the house, Liam burst out the French doors to hug her and pepper her with rapid-fire questions about his birthday party. He started to go inside with her, but Gideon called him over.

"Your mom and I need to talk to you, bud. You'll have to wait a few minutes to bother Erin."

Disappointment mingled with confusion, but he obeyed, reluctantly releasing Erin's hand and claiming the chair Matthew had abandoned.

"You want to tell him or should I?" Gideon asked Hannah.

"On Monday, I'm going to agree to your dad's custody arrangement."

"Does that mean…?"

"You'll be living with him full time during the week here in Sea Glass Cove and spending every other weekend with me. You're always happier with your dad, and I want that for you. Besides, our time together will be all the more precious and better for it."

Liam stared at her, dumbfounded. Then he glanced between them.

"I love you, Liam," Hannah said, her voice catching on the threat of tears. "I don't want to give you up, and I'm not, but this is what's best for you. Your dad's such a good dad and I'm…."

"A good mom who struggles a bit," Gideon supplied. And he meant it. "And one more thing. No more fighting. We're done with that, aren't we, Hannah."

She gave him a smile that conveyed a powerful gratitude entwined with equal parts regret and relief. Liam wormed his way around the table and dragged them together to hug them both at once.

"Are you happy?" Hannah asked uncertainly.

He only nodded, beaming with tears shining in his eyes.

"I love you, kiddo."

"I love you, too, Mom. I'm going to miss you, though."

"No you won't. Because we'll have more quality

time even if it's less in quantity. And Sea Glass Cove isn't that far from Beaverton—a couple hours, max. Anytime we get to missing each other too much, I can come see you, or your dad can bring you to see me."

Liam nodded and drew a shuddering breath, tightening his arms around his parents. Gideon's neck twinged, but he wasn't about to complain about it and ruin the most perfect moment the three of them had shared in... maybe ever.

"Happy birthday, Liam," Hannah whispered.

How long they stayed like that, Gideon couldn't say, but the spell broke when Matthew stepped outside and cleared his throat.

"I hate to interrupt this lovely picture, but you might want to put it on hold, Gideon."

There was a note in his father's voice that instantly put him on alert. "What's wrong?"

"Don't know that anything is, but Erin just left. Said she was going to go for a walk on the beach while you three talked."

Gideon frowned. It wasn't like Erin to wander off when there was work to be done. He glanced at Hannah, who shrugged.

"Maybe she was trying to give us some privacy."

He nodded, but if that were the case, his father wouldn't have intruded. "Did she say anything?"

"It wasn't what she said." Matthew flicked his gaze at Hannah in such a way to express his desire to speak to his son alone.

Gideon gave Liam's shoulder a squeeze and fol-lowed his father into the house. "If it wasn't what she said, what was it?"

"She looked—I don't know—like a woman tee-tering on the edge of some big decision."

"Why would she be?" Gideon asked more to him-self than to his father.

"Maybe you ought to give her a call. I don't think it's wise to give her too much time alone to think. She's the kind to talk herself into knots."

"Yes, she is, but I don't need to call. If she's up-set, I know where she went." Gideon embraced his fa-ther. "No fighting with Hannah while I'm gone. I don't want her to have an excuse to back out of her decision."

"What decision was that?"

"Giving me full custody of Liam."

He didn't give his father a chance to respond and didn't go back out to tell Hannah and Liam that he was leaving. Matthew could handle that. Instead, he raced upstairs, dressed in a rush, and dragged his hair back into a quick pony tail. He headed for the front door but hesitated with his hand on the knob. Then he strode across the living room to the den and pulled the ring box out of the desk drawer.

When he grabbed his keys, Shadow raced across the cottage, bouncing with excitement and wanting to go where ever he was.

"Not this time, pretty girl. We'll play on the beach later. I promise."

He dipped his head in acknowledgement of his father's knowing smile and slipped out the door. He had another promise to make first. Everything else could wait.

Seventeen

ERIN PERCHED ON THE LOG in front of her fort with her hands folded in her lap and leaned over her legs. For a while, she watched the waves lap at the beach, sparkling in the sun as it crested the forested hills guarding Sea Glass Cove. Her mind was empty of thought for a time, content to take in the familiar rhythm of the Pacific and the touch of thick salt air on her exposed face, but gradually, the issues that had driven her down to her fort seeped back in.

How had Gideon said it last night?

I swear, I've never seen this side of her.

And that smile when he'd said it....

He'd waited so long to see whatever it was Hannah had shown him last night, and Erin couldn't help but wonder how that would change things. After lying awake most of the night thinking about it, she'd almost convinced herself that it shouldn't. And when Gideon had kissed her with such unexpected pleasure despite her interruption of what was clearly an important conversation with Hannah, it was further confirmation that nothing needed to change just because his ex was finally stepping up. Then she'd glanced out the French doors just in time to see Liam's brilliant joy as he dragged his parents into a family hug.

That changed everything.

Liam needed his parents together. He *deserved* to have his family whole. And if Hannah truly was beginning to come around and be the parent Liam and Gideon needed her to be....

"Thought I'd find you here."

She pinched her eyes closed for a moment, then forced a smile as she turned her face to Gideon. Unlike the day she'd told him about the molestation and Chaz's cheating, there was no hesitation in him. He strode to her across the sand with his lips curved in amusement but concern shadowing those beautiful dark eyes. When he reached her, he gestured to the log, asking if he could sit with her.

She nodded. "Didn't take you long to find me. I've only been here a few minutes."

"For someone who is so refreshingly multi-faceted, you are surprisingly predictable." He paused a moment, then asked softly, "Everything all right?"

She opened her mouth to say yes, but the lie was sour in the back of her throat. "Um, I'm not sure."

"Okay...."

He picked up her hand and slipped his fingers between hers with such tenderness that, for a moment, she couldn't breathe and couldn't remember why everything wasn't all right.

"Want to talk to me about it?"

"Are we making a mistake?" she blurted.

"What do you mean?"

Shifting toward him, she noted the frown of confusion drawing his brows together. She started to give voice to the thoughts swirling through her mind, but they were too jumbled to grab on to. How could she explain that she was afraid them being together wasn't what was best for his son without sounding like she didn't care about what was best for Gideon?

Slowly, she finally said, "Hannah's finally starting to be what you needed her to be all along. And Liam.... You should've seen his smile out there on the deck with both his parents together and talking and not fighting. He was so happy, and it was beautiful. I can't take that away from him."

"Take what away from him? Erin, you aren't suggesting...." His voice trailed off, and disappointment flashed across his face. "No, we aren't making a mistake. And despite whatever you may think, there is no chance of reconciliation with Hannah."

"Not even if it's what's best for your son?"

"Not even then because it isn't. What's best for him is to have a happy father who doesn't fight constantly with his mother. And that's what would happen."

"But you're working things out with her."

"Erin. It's never going to happen. Do you know why I'm so sure?"

She shook her head.

"You."

She lowered her eyes, unable to withstand the unwavering confidence glowing in his eyes. "You've known me barely a month."

"Doesn't matter. Let me paint you a picture. It's a gorgeous summer night—the solstice, to be exact. Bonfires litter the beach from point to point, music and laughter drift across the sand, and it is as perfect a night as anyone could imagine. There's a group of people enjoying it all right here where you and I are sitting now. One of them is a single father watching this beautiful vixen teach his son the proper way to build a driftwood fort, and the joy on both their faces is so sublime and so precious. In those moments, this single father catches a glimpse of something he wasn't sure he'd ever find— the family he'd envisioned for his son with a woman who doesn't just humor him but enjoys his company and takes as much pleasure from this boy's happiness as his father does."

Erin closed her eyes to picture it and had no trouble. Liam had been so adorable and so enthusiastic, him and Daphne. It had been a perfect night, indeed, and she'd dreamt of it frequently in the weeks that followed.

"You are the reason I decided to file for full custody of Liam," Gideon continued quietly. "Did you know that?"

Jerking back, she stared at him. How could that possibly be true? He'd filed for custody in July—before they'd started dating.

"That night showed me..." He shook his head as a poignant smile graced his features. "...so much possibility. Things I'd stopped hoping for. How does that advice go? Don't invest in a relationship if you wouldn't want one like it for your child. Something like that. I wouldn't want Liam stuck in a relationship like I had with Hannah, settling for less than he deserves. That night, I saw what kind of woman I'd want for him. One who adores him and values what he has to offer and loves him, flaws and all." He took her face in his hands and brushed his thumbs over her cheeks, searching her eyes. "The kind I want for myself. You remember what you said to me at your mom's birthday? About what makes my heart beat?"

She nodded. "Your son. And I just want what's best for him, Gideon. I'm not doubting *you* at all. I know you love me."

"Silly woman," he murmured fondly. "You and me together is what's best for Liam. Because you love him and listen to him and give him what he *needs*. Because you make me happy. Because you make me want to be a better father and a better man."

Frowning, she shifted her gaze to the horizon as his words spun around with her fear that Liam needed his mother and father together in a dance that threatened to shift the world on its axis. She barely noticed Gideon shift his position even though he was sitting close enough that their bodies touched at several points.

"Maybe this will help you see how sure I am."

It took her a moment to understand that he was trying to show her something, and when she comprehended it, she glanced first at his face before realizing what he wanted to show her was in his hands.

Her breath sucked through her teeth. Resting in his palm was a ring box that he opened as soon as her eyes found it. She knew in a concrete way that it was an engagement ring cushioned so snuggly in the box, but her mind refused to latch onto the more abstract meaning of it.

"Gideon... what is this?"

"My mother's ring, intended since the day she died for the hand of the woman I want to marry. I never once considered it might ever grace Hannah's hand, but I knew it should be on yours that night we made love—

before we did. My father asked if I wanted him to bring it with him when he came down for Liam's birthday, and I said yes. Without hesitation."

"I don't understand. Are you proposing?"

"Sort of."

Suddenly overcome by the urge to laugh, she tilted her head. "How do you *sort of* propose?"

"Simple. *I* may be sure about us, but I don't think you are yet. And that's okay. Other men have put you through hell, and before you answer, I want you to believe without a single doubt that I won't ever be one of them. So this is a promise. A promise that I'll wait as long as you need me to. I know I still have a lot to prove. And if, when I have, you agree that this is forever, I'll know when you put the ring on your finger. And if you decide this isn't what you want, all you have to do is give it back, and I'll accept your decision."

"Just like that? No questions asked?"

"Well, I might ask questions." His lips twitched with humor. "I think I deserve that. But I won't try to push you into saying yes if it isn't what's in your heart."

When she made no move to take the ring, he took her hand, turned it over so her palm faced the sky, and settled the box—now closed again—into it.

"Think about it." He leaned forward to kiss her cheek. "I'll leave you to it. Because I need to get back up to the cottage. Dad and Hannah have a truce, but who knows what might set them off again."

Then he was gone, striding away across the sand and disappearing through the waving grasses of the dunes.

She stared after him for a long time until, once again, her gaze was drawn back to the sea. Not that she noticed more than the mesmerizing undulation of it; her attention was consumed by the small box in her hand.

He wanted to marry her.

On some level, she'd suspected he was heading in that direction. But... they'd been together less than a full month. How could he be so confident? Sure, his father had proposed to his wife after only two weeks, and their love was so strong he had not, in the nearly three decades since she'd died, found anyone who could compare. She didn't know much about their relationship, granted, but she didn't think they'd faced the same hurdles she and Gideon had and would for who knew how long, namely on her side. Sure, he'd been patient and understanding and willing to let her dictate the physical side of their relationship, and of course she adored him for that. And, yes, making love to him that night had been so much better than anything she'd shared with Chaz, and she found herself wanting to try things that had once made her squirm to even think of. But....

Her brows dipped as she searched for all the reasons why Gideon might turn away from her or why this delightful curiosity and desire might not last. She couldn't think of a single one.

She tried again.

But what?

The answer hung in the air, unanswered.

But he might tire of her? But he might wander in search of less inhibited companionship? Impossible. He'd spent years with Hannah, clinging to hope that she might someday become the partner he needed even though he'd suspected from the beginning that she never would be. In contrast, if he was to be believed, he'd felt such a powerful pull toward Erin at the summer solstice that it had convinced him to seek full custody of his son on the glimmer of a chance that a real love and a real family was on the horizon. Or, at the very least, meeting her had shown him that there was more out there for him and his son than what he'd settled for with Hannah for so long.

Erin lowered her gaze to the ring box, and she stroked it reverently for a while before compulsion drove her to open it. Maria St. Cloud's engagement ring was simple but elegant. Tentatively, she slipped it from its cushioning and held it up, admiring how it glistened and sparkled in the bright morning sun. Then, without contemplating her actions, she slid it onto the ring finger of her left hand.

Suddenly, everything became clear.

It was silly, really, how that simple motion brought everything into perfect balance.

She loved Gideon. She adored his son. She appreciated everything Gideon had already done to soothe her fears and heal her scars. He promised her that his son was in the best hands with her and with them together.

What else mattered?

Slowly, as if pushed by some unforeseen force, she rose from the log in front of her driftwood fort, glancing briefly back at her handiwork with a certainty that her days of seeking shelter in it and others like it were over.

She tucked the ring box in the pocket of her windbreaker and started toward her car in the northern parking area. Her confidence grew with each step and her face lifted until, when she reached her car, she was beaming. She drew her phone from her pocket, snapped a quick picture of the ring, and sent it to her brother with the message, *We're even. So tomorrow I'll tell you what really happened with Chaz.*

He was at his gallery, so she didn't expect him to respond, but her phone chimed only seconds later.

I told you so, he'd sent. A second message arrived. *Does it matter anymore what happened with Chaz?*

She pondered that for a moment, closed her eyes, and sighed—fully at peace. *No. It doesn't.*

I am thrilled for you, sis, and finished it with a heart emoji.

If it was possible, her smiled widened even more.

Gideon was in the kitchen of the cottage with his father, son, and Hannah working on Liam's birthday cake when she arrived. Quietly, she pulled him aside and handed him the ring box. His brows knitted together.

"Open it," she said.

He did, and his frown deepened. "Where's my mother's...?"

Coyly, she threaded the fingers of her left hand with those of his right and lifted both, tilting them toward his face so he could see.

He jerked his head up and stared at her for what felt like at least a minute. "Are you sure?"

She searched his eyes, and the hope that edged out the confidence inspired as much a sensation of power as of endearment. She nodded. "I don't need to think about it. I know you're the one."

He crushed her to him and let out a sigh of relief.

"Just so we're clear," she murmured, grinning, "that's a yes to your proposal."

Chuckling, he released her to pick up his son. "You hear that, bud? I asked Erin to marry me, and she said yes."

"What?!" the boy blurted. "Really?"

She laughed. "Yes, really."

"Oh, man!" He wrapped an arm around her neck, and Gideon draped an arm around her shoulders. "Best. Birthday. *Ever.*"

Matthew embraced them all and expressed his joy

at the announcement, and Shadow, sensing the excitement, pranced around them with her eyes happy and her ears alert. Even Hannah offered genuine if somewhat crestfallen congratulations as well.

"I'm curious," Gideon said after his father, Liam, and Hannah had gone back to the cake. "What made you decide you didn't need to think about this?"

"I realized that I've found what makes my heart beat."

He waited several moments before he gave in. "And that is…?"

She glanced at Liam and smiled. "Your sweet, beautiful son." Turning to Gideon again, she slipped her arms around his neck, rose up on her toes, and whispered against his lips, "But most especially… *you*."

* * * * *

ABOUT THE AUTHOR

Maren Ferguson is the "sweet" alter ego of *USA Today* bestselling author Suzie O'Connell, who is best known for the Northstar romances.

Though she is a self-professed mountain-loving nerd, she has a fair amount of salt water in her veins, courtesy of her "salty dog" grandfather, and once in a while, she gets to craving the crashing ocean surf. It was during one of these episodes that the Sea Glass Cove series was conceived.

Suzie has been writing stories for as long as she can remember, and it shouldn't come as any surprise that her first story, written (and illustrated) way back in second grade, was about the mouse who went to the sea.

When she isn't writing, you'll probably find her in the mountains with a camera in hand and enjoying the beauty of Montana with her husband Mark, their daughter Maddie, and their golden retriever Reilly. You might even find her—on her rare trips to the coast—getting in touch with her inner pirate. Just kidding. Sort of.

To find out more about Suzie and her books, stop by her websites:

www.marenferguson.com
www.suzieoconnell.com

71263453R00137

Made in the USA
Middletown, DE
21 April 2018